Stephen Phillips was born in Clevedon Somerset, UK, in 1944. He is married with two children and five grandchildren. He has written art criticism for Artspace, poetry, a few short stories, and several course programmes professionally, as a 3D art and design lecturer, and Art School head. He is a practising artist and educator and has travelled extensively throughout Europe and the UK in self-converted camper vans.

To Mrs P.

Stephen Phillips

Q

By All and Every Means

AUSTIN MACAULEY PUBLISHERS™

LONDON · CAMBRIDGE · NEW YORK · SHARJAH

A CIP catalogue record for this title is available from the British Library.

ISBN 9781528942386 (Paperback)
ISBN 9781528971126 (ePub e-book)

www.austinmacauley.com

First Published (2019)
Austin Macauley Publishers Ltd
25 Canada Square
Canary Wharf
London
E14 5LQ

This is a work of fiction with no political, religious or anti-Semitic intent, as I have no abiding interest in politics or religion or race whatsoever.

The Prologue

From Wikipedia: Q source: also, Q document or Q.

Q: is the hypothetical written source for the Gospel of Matthew and the Gospel of Luke.

Q: is short for the German: *Quelle* or 'source' and is defined as the common material found in Matthew and Luke, but not in Mark. This ancient text supposedly contained the logia or quotations from Jesus. Archaeologist and theologians have been searching for this documentation in any form for centuries. Academic opinion is divided, but many a learned case has been made for the pre-existence of Q even if no longer extant.

Professor Lochlan Majewski was expecting a visitor, who had phoned the previous day to arrange an informal meeting concerning a project of international importance, in which, he said, Lochlan may have an essential role. He was not too excited as he was often asked to add his support to global concerns, but he had wondered what possible project an eminent Rabbi may proffer. The bell rang and he buzzed the external door open to let him into the communal hallway. Lochlan stood at the top of the stairs offering a welcome, to a tall middle-aged man, larger in the girth than he had expected. Resting on the second of the communal landings, he called up to his host.

"You may know me from the television Professor Lochlan: Rabbi Simon Cohen." Lochlan walked down a staircase to meet him, and warmly clasped the Rabbi's moist hand in greeting.

"Yes of course, but from the radio, maybe, but do come up and take a seat and I'll perk the coffee, you said black, no sugar?"

"No, white usually. No sugar please and thank you for your time."

"You're most welcome, Rabbi. Do go up."

Professor Lochlan's apartment was a testament to his travels for academic research. Numerous face masks from all corners of the southern hemisphere stared down from the picture rail into the large main room, where every available surface, exhibited curios. More than a hundred, small carved hardwood figures, and a greater number of intriguing ceramics – some containing large plants – were crammed onto any horizontal space. Indian fabrics curtained the high windows offering a defuse sunlight that danced on several Afghani carpets interrupting the sweep of the wooden floor. Also, confusingly, there were numerous working clocks, – each telling a different time – and several shelved alcoves, fully booked, or packed with vinyl records and compact discs. All non-shelved wall space presented an eclectic taste in paintings and prints.

There were two oversized sofas, one was conventional, facing a small television, the other consisted of a double bed mattress, on a low platform, where a variety of large kelim cushions flopped invitingly. Rabbi Cohen was only too aware, though both sofas were undoubtedly comfortable, he would need a helping hand to return to the vertical. Deciding instead, to sit on one of the unrelated dining chairs, resting his elbows on the large polished table, clasping his hands together, greeting himself.

"My word," he exclaimed, "what an extraordinary room, I guess many of the things on display have been procured from your travels."

"Yes, many are from my research journeys, but not all. The clocks are from the local 'flea market' and show the actual time in the many countries where I have friends or business. I find it useful when I need to communicate internationally. Saves checking. The one over there is on New York time, and this one here is Auckland."

"They are, no doubt, most interesting, Professor, but I must say, I just could not live with the clutter. I try to live a simple life with fewer possessions. One never can know when one may move on to one's maker."

"Yes, well that's true, although it's a philosophy not entirely shared by all religious leaders I believe. However, the clutter to which you refer drove Dianne, my last girlfriend, mad."

"I must say I do sympathise; however, we may assume from your well-regarded published work, Professor, that such a cluttered room exhibits an ordered mind, and a minimalist interior a dissolute one, perhaps?"

"Ordered and logical; and therefore, not religious, as you possibly gathered from our conversation yesterday. I was most bemused by your phone call, but you must know, I practice no faith whatsoever."

"Yes, yes, quite; I know, you were most emphatic, but as a Jew one still may not be impartial."

"That's as maybe; but do continue."

"Well, before we can proceed, I really need your assurance that you will not divulge our conversation to anyone, anyone at all, not even to your partner."

"No problem, as from yesterday, I don't have a partner."

Rabbi Cohen glanced around the large room remarking on several female items.

"Dianne is coming for her things at the weekend."

"Oh dear, I am sorry, we could do this another time."

"No, no, I'm good, no worries, I've been there before; and she was never long term. Fire away as I'm intrigued by your insistence on secrecy."

"Quite; quite; yes, I'm sure you are. Okay. As you are probably aware, I have a visible or more accurately, respected, media profile and I'm representing a small collective of mixed faith brethren, who have asked me to discuss an academic project which could turn out to be somewhat important to you, for the rest of your life. You may well wince, Professor, a bit over the top, I know, but we have need of your considerable expertise and invaluable practical experience for a major, but nonetheless discreet project based on a recent archaeological discovery. The few people with the knowledge of the contents of these ancient objects are sworn to keep its secrets, to avoid adverse publicity. Do you see?"

"Not really, no, how come? And call me Lochlan, please."

"Now this is an important new discovery. These ancient texts require verification, eventually, as they may possibly be contemporary with the apostles."

"Really?" he queried. "Sounds interesting. Concurrent, you think? On stone, vellum, lead?"

"Tablets. Incised clay tiles. We can refer to them as tablets."

"That's great news Rabbi, but why phone me?"

"Well," Rabbi Simon Cohen hesitated, as if remembering something. "We are very familiar with your restorative work on the Gaelic Book of Kells, and of course more recently, the Garima Gospels and your scholarly verification of their earlier date. I have also been reading your book on the Tapa bark paper prints and images from the South seas, and their conservation and relevance to ritual and belief. Polynesia and Fiji through to New Zealand, I believe. Fascinating stuff, mulberry bark paper."

"And breadfruit parchment. Not exactly a bedtime read I suspect. I loved that period of research, for Auckland University, lovely islands, friendly spiritual peoples, they were so pleased that I took an interest."

"Yes, I'm sure they were. Didn't Auckland give you an honorary doctorate?"

"Aha, have you been reading my CV?"

"Well, yes. We have taken an interest in your background."

"That sounds ominous."

"No. No; not at all, Professor. The Brethren were also impressed by your command of languages and your literary competence. We always undertake a thorough evaluation of a candidate, because; if you undertake and complete this momentous project, there may be more than excellent remuneration. There could be further accolades, maybe, even a Knighthood in the offing. One just doesn't know."

Lochlan was speechless, he wasn't naïve, he was conversing with one of the establishment (if measured by their potential influence) he knew, or at least, surmised, that 'things' were sometimes done this way, although he clearly understood, if Rabbi Cohen was serious, then this was big, very big, and potentially not without consequences. He felt like giggling; he was certainly troubled.

"What Project Rabbi? And we, who are we exactly? And please, it's Lochlan."

"I represent a few eminent Christian brethren who have the interests of our homeland and our people at heart, and they have confided in me, and I have agreed, on pain of death, you understand, to pursue their ideas to a conclusion."

"On pain of death. On pain of death," Lochlan exclaimed dismissively. "Now come off it. On pain of death. Really!" Rabbi Cohen grimaced. "I'm sorry, I don't want to seem disrespectful, but, really."

"You have to realise, Professor Lochlan, what we are hoping to achieve, could, or more aptly, would, change the course of history, especially of our people," Rabbi Cohen bristled and said this with undisguised irritation.

"No, well, sorry, yes, I am listening, I am," Lochlan deferred as he now realised he may well be party to some information of import. "Are you referring to something like the DSS?"

"No, not really, as the Dead Sea Scrolls pre-date Christ as you are of course well aware. I am still referring to a recent find of sorts, contemporary with our Lord's ministry."

"I did say on the phone that he is not *my* Lord; Rabbi," Lochlan emphasised *my,* "and the actual dates of some DSS finds have been shown to be near contemporary with Christ's ministry, have they not? But do continue."

Rabbi Cohen leant forward to speak as if there was someone else listening in the room, lowering his voice, to a confiding tone.

"Well," Rabbi Cohen hesitated, dramatically. "We believe that we may have found Q."

"No way!"

"Yes, on incised clay tablets. Yes; in fact, we are certain that we have."

"No! Wow! No, not the Four Apostle's common source? Are you sure? Certain, really, Q," Rabbi Cohen nodded. "Jesus! Where? How? Now I am interested, how cool is that? I can see why your brethren wanted to keep that quite until they are certain; tell me more. This may explain Mark's biblical verbosity once and for all. I knew it. I knew it."

"Well, we have noted that you have made strong arguments in favour of Q in your Doctrinal Thesis."

"Yes, the existence of Q is common sense. *We* have always believed it was out there somewhere. Brilliant. That is excellent. Wow-wee."

"Yes, our people are very excited at the possibilities."

"There is more coffee, although I am plum out of milk."

"No thanks, I'm fine, although a bit peckish. Can I treat you? We could go to the Thai, they do a splendid light lunch I hear."

"They most certainly do. Let's do that, I am intrigued, to say the least, but troubled by your allusion to absolute secrecy. I mean, 'on pain of death', but now I am beginning to understand; that's hot news."

"Well, you had better not call me Rabbi in the restaurant, I guess."

"Simon it is then."

***

As they walked, the character actor Paul Smith was a little more relaxed while playing a Rabbi, as he believed his subterfuge was working. Lochlan was wondering why we say, 'plum out of milk', and the Rabbi, 'our peoples'? And did 'our peoples' mean all Christians or his peoples?

As they entered the restaurant, they were greeted most sweetly, by a diminutive Thai waitress, as elegant and as perfectly formed as the purple flower in her hair. She showed them to a table.

"What shall we eat? You use this place a good deal, I believe, don't you?"

"Yes, I do, often. I guess your people have been monitoring my life style as well?"

Lochlan didn't expect an answer, the openly-contrived look of innocence he received from his fellow diner said everything.

"What do you fancy, Simon?"

"I guess it depends more on our need for conversation, don't you find? Some food makes it just not possible to eat and talk. Like spaghetti, peas, or soup. "

"Pity, I was going for a Tom Yam for starters."

"Okay, I love Thai soups, Tom Yam it is, I will refrain from answering any more questions."

Of course, they talked and talked, and after some time, it became clear to Lochlan that he was being offered work in his field of expertise that could be both challenging and lucrative.

He still had no real notion of the exact task or tasks, although he understood it involved working with scripts that were contemporary with Christ's ministry and would require verification. The Project was expected to last several months, and he was also told that he would need a sabbatical period to get started, but then the work, research etcetera, could be undertaken at home, or so he was led to believe. He would have to swear not to mention The Project's content to anyone. That was made clear, but he understood that if the media got hold of the story, it would be rubbished or exaggerated to the death by the *media*. It sounded all a bit clandestine and suspect, but on the other hand, he was intrigued, and subscribed to the possibility that he would be exonerated for his part intuitive, yet well researched and argued publication, on the origins and evidence for the likely pre-existence of Q.

Lochlan tried to appear interested, but not over enthusiastic, as no contractual details were mentioned. After agreeing to meet again the following day to give him time to evaluate the proposition, Rabbi Cohen had left by taxi for another appointment.

Possibly for a snooze, Lochlan thought. He stayed on, for a beer or two whilst perusing a populist novel he presumed a customer had left.

***

"Hello, I'm Rebecca, Rebecca Stein: I just sort of wondered what you thought about the book. The one you're reading, as I saw the cover, and wondered."

Lochlan stared at her as he tried desperately to recall a foreign student of that name and features, he may have taught.

"I'm not making much sense, am I?"

She was beautiful he noticed, as he struggled to place her accent, possibly French Canadian, he thought.

"I'm not making much sense. Sorry?"

"You want my opinion?"

"Yes, well, something like that. Yes. What do you think?"

"I think that it's quite possibly a load of bollocks." He regretted his statement immediately, as he could see from her expression, she had thought him abrupt, even rude.

"Really?" She was unnerved, unsure and flushed.

"Yes really." He was overcome by her beauty, and not making much sense himself. As he indicated that she should sit with him, she sidled into a seat at his table.

"I can't put that in my thesis," she said through a broad smile.

My word: but she is quite gorgeous, he thought. Student, so maybe single.

"Have you seen the film of this book," he enquired, flummoxed, not knowing what to say.

"No, I haven't, but I have been meaning to. How about you?"

"Me neither, not that I particularly wish to. Would you like a drink?" as he asked her, he realised that he had been staring at her cleavage and the lightly tanned beauty of her skin. He determined to prolong the encounter.

"Er, yes, but, what's the time?" she said glancing at the wall clock. "Shall we go? We could just make the matinee. It's on in your local multi-screen."

"Is it? Okay, but it would be full of kids, it's half-term." Lochlan suggested, panicking, as he realised, she was serious. She picked up her bag, slung it over her shoulder, gestured to

Lochlan to get up, as she held his hand and pulled him through to the restaurant exit. He signalled, from the street, to James, the restaurant owner, that he would pay his beer bill next time.

Lochlan was trying hard to keep up as they both ran across the park towards the cinema, arriving just in time to occupy seats. She was fit, in all senses of the word he noticed, and quite tall, with those long strides. He had little time to consider this unusual situation as the film started while he was still gasping for breath and wiping sweat off his brow with the back of his sleeve. Breathing in deeply, he smelt her. A moist, warm, earthy, yet distinctly feminine perfume.

All through the film he turned occasionally to glimpse her profile, such a fine young head, and long neck, he thought. He noticed the elegant fingers of her hands were long and smooth and sported what appeared to be a diamond wedding ring, although, placed on the wrong finger. Divorced maybe, he thought, but he couldn't even discern a mark or indentation from a previous ring. He couldn't believe his luck. It was unusual for a pretty female, well, any female, to make a beeline for him as he usually had to make the running and bamboozle them with his sharp wit and humour, or so he believed. Confusingly, it was the second time a young woman had entered his life recently and made all the running. Literally this time. He wasn't going to change his aftershave anytime soon, he decided.

* * *

On the previous occasion, Dianne had approached him at the University, introducing herself as a journalist that wanted to write a profile on him for 'BAM', the Body-Art Magazine she represented, as her article placed an emphasis on the ethnic tattoo designs by the inhabitants of the Polynesia Archipelago. He was flattered, but extremely busy with the new student intake, and unable to find time for several weeks during the day, he jokingly suggested – as she was young, blonde and beautiful – that it would be more beneficial to both of them, if she moved in to his place to take notes on his interests and lifestyle, giving her his UCL business card, which had his home address. He had a few of these cards designed and printed with his numerous qualifications and published academic works listed. These were distributed at conferences and seminars, although he had passed most of them to London taxi drivers when he was often too inebriated to talk or remember his postcode. Lochlan was being dismissive and thought no more about the incident.

Dianne rang his door-bell that evening, and he ran down the stairs to answer the door. He was speechless. She just stood there, holding on to her luggage case, expectantly. He had thought no more about her, thinking that she dismissed his joke in passing, as he had not been serious. She seemed so upset by his indifference that he felt sorry for her and invited her in to see his apartment and some of his photographs and drawings of Maori body tattoos.

Lochlan was bemused and disorientated by the evening's end, as after much talk and wine and a revealing yet tentative perusal of her own tattoos, she emptied her Louis Vuitton case of clothes, evidently assuming they would be sleeping together. Not only taking up half the space in his little wardrobe, but more than half the space in his bed, without even asking. She just made herself at home. He wasn't comfortable with the situation. He even considered the possibility that she was homeless and desperate, although he knew the price of her suitcase could pay his rent for a few months. After several days' cohabitation, he was scheming to get Dianne to leave, but he couldn't bring himself to tell her.

He often slept alone in his apartment and was not used to seeing another person's toiletries in his bathroom, or, witnessing the swift demise of the toilet paper. She also had a compulsion to rearrange his various collections into neat lines or regular patterns. His scatter cushions were regimented in a neat terrace on the sofa backs and even his CDs, previously organised by genre, were sorted in alphabetical order. Afterwards, Lochlan couldn't find anything. His cleaner was disturbed as there was nothing to clean. Dianne had a precise cleaning routine making sure Lochlan put everything away, especially in the kitchen. He told his mum, sarcastically, that it was like living at home again. She was pleased for him and asked to meet her.

Dianne enquired into his background, his finances, his relationships with his colleagues, his students, and even questioned the regulars at The Dolphin Pub he frequented. He seemed to be in a subordinate position all the time, forced to yield to the power of someone who remained silent as he rambled on. Asking questions, without responding to his, while he revealed his innermost thoughts. He felt more emotionally naked than she was physically most of the time, although he felt more comfortable when she wore clothes, if Mel, his cleaner, was expected. He was unnerved by Dianne's accoutrements, as he referred to her all-over body tattoo, and numerous piercings with rings or studs: everywhere.

***

As they left the cinema, Rebecca hooked her arm into Lochlan's and moved closer.

"You know this book cannot be on any academic reading list, you must know that? Not even for an American institution," he said, glancing up at her whilst tapping the book in his pocket.

"Yes, I know, I've been rumbled. You looked artistic and interesting with your spiked hair. I have only just arrived in London from the States and didn't know anyone, and I didn't want to eat alone. You know what I mean? It's easier for men, they can be on their own in a restaurant without being thought to be 'easy'." He knew what she meant by 'easy' of course, but he was wondering, as she had seen him sitting alone, whether it maybe reciprocal.

"I came over to study at your lovely Courtauld Institute."

"What specifically?"

"European Art before the First World War and call me Becky."

"That's not specific, that's major Becky." There was an awkward silence and no answer. "What did you think of the film?" he said suddenly.

Rebecca wasn't sure what to say as she loved the film as much as she thought most of the schoolchildren of all ages in the cinema seemed to, but she was determined to ingratiate herself.

"I loved the New Zealand landscape," she said

"I loved its wildernesses when I lived there," he said casually.

"Oh, you have lived there? I didn't know."

"Why should you?" he asked indignantly.

Lochlan walked Rebecca to the Underground Station and they parted, pleased with themselves, but for very different reasons. As he walked the long way home, he pondered on the day.

Lochlan was troubled that she had been so forward, but he was sufficiently arrogant to consider, as an Academic and intellectual, he may well look interesting – although deluded, as he was twice as old as most students, but tried to dress and act their age – after all, he thought, even Miller got lucky with Monroe. He felt privileged to have spent some time with such a lively exquisite beauty, while noticing an inherent deep sadness in her doe-like eyes. He threw the book into a general waste bin. *I should have recycled it,* he thought – when later he passed a Paper Bank bin. – although most of the content has already been recycled, he surmised. That night he fantasised about her; Rebecca was clearly sat on his face in cyber-space and as Dianne was easily forgotten, all was right with the world.

***

Rebecca's phone rang.

"Hi, Uncle Paul, did you enjoy playing a Senior Rabbi?"

"Not really, I was more nervous than my first Malvolio at Stratford."

"Well, I guess you weren't given such good lines."

"That's very true. I kept calling him Professor as his first name slipped my mind. How did our Professor react to your intrusion Becky?"

"He was fine. He seems taken with me. We went to see the film you suggested, as he picked up the book you left behind, as you thought he might. Although there was no mention of another date, but I will bump into him again after your next meeting, I'm sure."

"Yes, you will. He suggested the Bikers Café in the High Street, Hackney. It's an awful place, but I must play along, I am meeting him there tomorrow midday, to comprehensively reinforce The Brethren's absolute need for secrecy and his perpetual silence, that's my task. Could you catch his eye after I leave and glean his reaction?"

"Sure, will do, Uncle."

"How was the film?"

"Noisy."

"Do you think he has taken the bait?"

"Hard to tell, he never mentioned you or how he had spent his day, when I asked him. Also, he said that he worked as a conservationist, which could have meant wildlife, not manuscripts, but he didn't elaborate, even when pushed. He seems to be a steady guy."

"Did you like him?"

"Yes, I think I did."

"I did, also, Becky, although he is rather eccentric, don't you think? With that hair and those combat trousers. He didn't seem at all phased by my visit or my insistence that he remained stumm."

"Perhaps he doesn't really believe you. I'll sign off uncle, I'm dog-tired."

***

"Hello again, Simon, coffee, tea, pain raison? Do take a seat in the bay window area as it's usually quieter there for a chat."

"A patisserie in a biker's café, whatever next? Professor. Just 'builders tea' please, no sugar, thanks."

The Continental Café had been a Mecca for motor cyclists for decades although the clientele had always disowned a nomenclature that harked back to the early years of the twentieth century. The Café became an informal meeting room for the local 'Bikers' as they preferred to be called, including an offshoot of The Hells Angels, known as The Hackney Harriers. The walls behind the serving area were densely covered in a few hundred motorbike memorabilia, that included logos, insignia and ephemera collected over the years and a large notice board near the kitchen area that was covered in postcards and photos from a myriad of 'Biking' events, both home and abroad. There was a separate board with the occasional advertisement for motorbike sales, group notices; including a request for female members, preferably blondes.

The floor was overlaid with a chequerboard of vinyl tiles in yellow and black, although the floor area in front of the pay desk and ordering area, had been worn to a uniform grey. The chairs were original Eames laminated plywood with tubercular metal supports and the tables were the original Ercol Formica topped tables that had been there for years. Even the lighting celebrated the bland intensity of neon. A blue light box in the kitchen frazzled the flies which remained dormant, until their dry lifeless bodies were blown away when both doors to the premises were opened in unison.

Lochlan collected the tray and sat down opposite as Rabbi Cohen tapped two sweeteners into his tea from a small container.

"They used to put the sugar directly into the tea-urn in here, and that's not so long ago."

"Goodness me, Lochlan, did they? How ghastly, especially for diabetics, don't you think? I'm a bit pushed for time as I have ordered a taxi, although I presume it can wait in the motorbike park. It's good to meet you again. Now. We are hoping for a decision from you soon. Have you given the Brethren's offer and The Project more thought, Professor?"

"Yes, of course, I have considered all aspects and possible outcomes, and I fully appreciate the need for secrecy. I am of course intrigued to say the least, but I find this talk about 'on pain of death', and a KBE well, a bit, you know, outrageous. It makes me question your sincerity, as I have been thinking, '*you cannot be serious*'."

"You smirk professor and belittle the context and the need for secrecy. This is a momentous project, quite possibly life changing, not just for you, but maybe millions of people. You have been very dedicated in your work and pushed the boat out for quite frankly, little reward, and the financial encouragement for your work on Q's verification would be considerable, you understand?"

"I get by."

"I'm sure you do, and so does Prince Charles, but with a little more ease and comfort I suspect. Many have been ennobled for their secret work, diplomatic, that sort of thing, who, due to their clandestine activity, are not household names, yet, enjoy a similar level of comfort to his nibs. Not all keep quiet of course, there are no guarantees."

"What happens to the snitchers? I'm most reluctant to ask?"

"Some hide in the Australian outback with the camels. All get their comeuppance in time."

"Not all, surely? Some must make their getaway, do a *Lord Lucan* surely?" Lochlan suddenly thought of the comedy film

'Aeroplane' and the line *'And stop calling me Shirley'*. He smiled to himself and giggled.

"The oath of silence is to be taken seriously," Simon said, slightly nonplussed. "Do you imagine that all conspiratorial theorists are a bit loopy? Most are, but not all, I am led to believe. Perhaps some accidents are inevitable. What do you think would happen if the UN's Chief Inspector of weapons of mass destruction was asked by a senior member of the US administration to verify that there was clear evidence of WMD in a despot's country, after allowing US military staff to plant the evidence?" Rabbi Cohen was getting quite animated, pressing his ample stomach into the table as he moved his head closer to Lochlan to emphasise his point. "What if he, or she, was asked to falsify the documentary evidence and he, or she, said emphatically, No Way. What if he was so outraged that he threatened to break the story to the media, to blow the whistle on the whole dam deal. Presidents would be discredited, governments would fall, the enemy, would dance for joy. What do you think might happen to The Chief Inspector if he, or she, insisted on whistle blowing and denigrating the most powerful and richest nation in the history of the earth?"

"He, or she, would be 'rubbed out' I guess, is that the jargon?" Lochlan asked nervously.

"Yes, Professor, he would have a timely accident *tout suite.*"

"Is that what happened?"

"I would like to think not, no, that was conjecture, a w*hat if.*"

"What are you trying to tell me?" Lochlan said with a degree of agitation. "Are you suggesting something may happen to me if I don't play ball and verify Q. Is that it? What sort of offer is that?"

"No, no, no. Not so, Lochlan." Rabbi Cohen relaxed, smiled and sat back in his chair. "I just wanted to make it absolutely clear to you that in taking on this exciting and important Project, which we, The Brethren, are sincerely hoping you will, you are agreeing to absolute secrecy; absolute, for life; for your life, do you understand; for your life, and if you are unable or unwilling to take on The Project you are still forbidden to divulge anything about it to anyone once you knew the details. In other words, now that you are aware that we have discovered Q, you are already compromised Professor."

Lochlan was a bit knocked back by the Rabbi's forcefulness, and was speechless and looked anxious, as he took in the significance of what was said, fully aware of the importance of their Q discovery.

Rabbi Simon Cohen, aka, the established character actor Paul Smith (who had been recruited and briefed for this role by The Brethren) had hoped for this reaction from Lochlan, because it meant that he had convinced his charge, The Project was authentic, and Q had been discovered.

"There are many avenues of vested interest in this Project, Professor, and not all are heaven sent or destined for that place in the hereafter. Have I made myself clear?"

"Abundantly Rabbi, as in, *on pain of death*," Lochlan replied with more than a touch of sarcasm.

"Quite so, Professor, look, think it over for a few days until the end of the week, then we will send a car for you, to a place to be agreed, on Friday. You can then meet the rest of the team and learn more about the whole scheme. We will show you some of the research and outline what's required of you and from you. I think we have established just how secret this Project will have to be to protect Q, and that you will be paid handsomely and want for nothing in the future. If you don't want to proceed, (he gave Lochlan his business card) just phone this number and inform my secretary that you are withdrawing. Just say that you are withdrawing your application, he will note your decision, and nothing will be said. You will hear no more from us again. Although, you may, if you let it be known, to anybody, anyone at all, that we have found Q. This find is too important to be thwarted by a loose tongued individual. In that event..." Rabbi Cohen paused, placing his body and face up close again, lowering his tone, to add an austere theatrical emphasis. "We may then need to contact you to express our definite disapproval and concern. The clue is in *definite*. I hope you understand."

***

After the Rabbi had left the Café, a pensive and troubled Lochlan continued to sit at their table, casually looking out of the Café window. He was idly turning over Rabbi Cohen's business card, wondering why it had been printed cheaply via a free business card company. Perhaps he's not the real deal, he queried, there is something about his voice that's not sincere, and *thwarted* is not exactly reverential pc, so maybe. Then he saw her, Rebecca, walking on the opposite side of the street. He shot out of the Café and hailed her with a loud piercing two fingered whistle. She acknowledged him, with a fluttering excitable wave and crossed the road, but with some difficulty, attempting to cross while a convoy of 'Bikers' passed.

"Hey. Hello again," she said with false surprise.

He put his arm around her waist, a friendly gesture, that also gathered her towards the Café door.

"I'm in this Café, do join me? Say yes, I have just had a truly awful meeting with the devil incarnate I do believe."

"I'm supposed to be doing the weekly shop, but yeah, why not, you do look a bit troubled."

He held the door open and she caught his warm masculine smell as she passed him to enter. In the Café, men noticed her, women stared.

"Wow! What a great café. It's so fifties retro, wow!"

"It's not retro, it's just old, it's been here forever. I used to come here when I was a kid and play on the pinball machines, they don't have them anymore, brilliant time wasters. What would you like?"

"A Diet Coke please. Who was the devil incarnate?"

"Oh, just a potential employer, with an offer of a future lucrative life-threatening assignment."

"Life-threatening, are you a spy?" she said jokingly, as they sat down, "And who's the devil?"

"Ah! Just one of Gods representatives who made me an offer that I shouldn't refuse, not exactly a horse's head in the bed, more like a 'Catch-22' conundrum."

"What's the catch?"

"Well, you may ask." He paused for a second. Should I have this conversation? He wondered, although I need a sounding board, someone who, quite honestly, has no reason to feel involved, someone who I may not see again. "I have been offered a chance to undertake an interesting academic assignment that could make my name, as I understand it, and my fortune; although nobody will be aware of my contribution, except those few eminent persons, who commission whatsoever it is."

"You don't know what The Project may be?"

"No way Jose."

"And the catch?" Rebecca knew nothing about the actual Project, but she understood that an important archaeological find they called Q, appertaining to Christ's ministry, had to be endorsed by Professor Lochlan. Her uncle had told Rebecca, her job was to befriend, listen, encourage and persuade. Reporting any instance, no matter how trivial, that may abort The Project. Especially if Lochlan mentioned anything to do with Q, breaching confidentiality. The deadline for his agreement was Sunday. She knew she only had a few days.

"Well the catch is, that I am dammed if I do and I may be dammed if I don't."

Rebecca was expecting Lochlan to be confused, as she knew for his role, her uncle, the actor Paul Smith (while impersonating Rabbi Simon Cohen) had to be emphatic about Lochlan's secrecy and the consequences if he divulged The Project's content to anyone. She didn't know what the 'consequences' may be at this juncture. Her uncle had only said they were dire.

"Come on let's go to a pub, you know this area, take me to a good pub, I just love your pubs."

"They're all dives around here."

"Then take me to a dive, whatever that is. Is it 'a spit and sawdust'? My ex took me to one when I was over here a few years ago. It was full of men, very earthy, I loved it."

She refers to her ex, he noted and to *The Project,* which is strange as I don't think I did, but I guess an academic assignment is a project. However, Lochlan dismissed his concerns as he found her most charming, sensual and stimulating company and determined to prolong their acquaintance. He took her to three pubs, shouting over the music about academia, gay rights and American foreign policy, while playing pool (which she let him win) and darts (which he won) and dominoes with his friends. In each pub he seemed to know several people, of all nationalities, male and female, and they greeted him with warmth and enthusiasm. Rebecca was demonstrably keen on him and for his part, he was ebullient and upbeat as he could see that the confused pub regulars were wondering if he, Lochlan, had pulled another model.

They ate in the Thai Orchid, nearby his apartment, as Rebecca had missed her 'food shop' and told him, she was famished. Afterwards, because it was so late and Rebecca lived in Marylebone, which he suggested was too far to travel across town from the restaurant; and as she had consumed too much alcohol. She stayed the night at his place.

***

Paul Smith, aka Simon Cohen, phoned his niece.

"Well done Rebecca, good work my girl. How was it for you?"

"No details uncle, you always want the juicy details, don't you? Mostly we slept."

"I know your *mostly* young lady: poor man."

"He is most definitely hooked, but I think that he is going to be hard to play as we only have until the weekend really."

"I know, not enough time, maybe, but we must try. Okay? Now, Becky, what we would like you to do tomorrow, is to help us consolidate the appreciation of his immediate ancestry, if that's okay? We have completed his family tree, a profile of his ancestry, so to speak, and we are sending it over by courier today as agreed, so you may peruse the contents with him, rather than on screen, more intimate, we think. Are you still there, at his place?"

"Yes, under his pink duvet."

"Pink. That's a bit worrying, pink, okay. Any more to add?"

"Only that I think that he may be cleverer than we think, or your Brethren think."

"How come? I mean academically he is a bloody brain box. Double first Oxford and all that, speaks several languages fluently, except English of course."

"No, uncle, I mean; more switched on, more aware, sharp, clued up, street wise. He trounced his friends and me at dominoes, which I always thought was a game of chance, but obviously not: and you never mentioned his gambling at which, so his friends say, he is often a winner, horses mostly. He certainly had a grasp of US politics, interstate and internationally. Anyway, he speaks English perfectly well, he is after all British, isn't he?"

"I mean his use of slang… 'No worries' … 'You guys' … 'That's cool'… And his intonation rises at the end of every sentence: awful, he's definitely not fluent Becky."

"Very funny," Rebecca said blandly, "You are an old stuff shirt. What an amazing pad, all that ethnic stuff and did you go to his loo? It's extraordinary, all the walls are covered with flattened drinks cans, the beer cans that get squashed under vehicles. The ones you see flattened in the road. 'Road Kill' he calls them. They are from all over the world, he collects them. He is quite an oddball."

"I'm not surprised, he is rather 'youthful' for his age, don't you think? Still, have a good day tomorrow and let me know ASAP, his response to the ancestral profile we have sent. Try and get him to read all and access the web pages, and do stress the loyalty angle, be subtle, but we were hoping he may have some prior knowledge and an innate sense of allegiance as you and I do. It would benefit all of us if he recognised his roots and came on board as a convert so to speak."

"A.O.K, will do. I'm being cautious, but he seems a regular guy."

"Are you sure?"

"Yes; I'm kinda certain. He hasn't mentioned Dianne as you thought, or her particular interests, although I'm hoping he may surprise me."

"You're incorrigible Becky."

"As you should know uncle."

***

Lochlan went downstairs to the front door to sign for the parcel that Rabbi Simon had promised. He had always wanted to research into his ancestry, out of curiosity, to some extent, but mainly to see if there may be an inheritance languishing, with his name on it. He often dreamt of inheriting a Scottish castle, or enough money, or both, to get out of teaching. A profession from which he was feeling alienated due to 'shed loads' of government interference and creeping privatisation, as he saw it. He was also finding that his students were more self-centred than he was, ever; or so he believed.

They reviewed the parcel's contents together, an endeavour that led him to be quiet, for some time. Sensing a conflict in his manner and knowing from her own research into her ancestry that his may contain some disturbing information, she asked if he was fully aware of his Jewish ancestry.

"Yes, of course, as my grandmother and grandfather were Jewish, they arrived in the UK from Poland, just before the war, as did his brother. The fact that my mother was of Jewish parentage I knew, but I never knew we had *lost* so many relatives, I just assumed that they were somewhere in central Europe."

"You must ask your mother all about this when you next see her."

"I, we, the family, have often asked her, as she still has an agile memory, but she is not forthcoming. I'm not even sure why I have my dad's surname. I am seeing her on the weekend, so I will try again."

"This weekend?" she queried. He nodded.

"Yes, is there a problem?"

"Ere, No," she said, changing the subject. "Why would your employer research your family tree in such detail, don't you think it's taking staff profiling, a bit too far?"

"Potential employer," he corrected immediately. "Yes, it is a wee bit unnerving, but the Brethren obviously want to convince me of my duty, my Jewish duty, and I am a bit troubled by that. For a start my father was a non-practising Catholic, and he was never married to my mother. But, even if my dad was the Pope, I'm pretty sure that I would still have skipped church."

"That's the wrong religion and you know it," she said with a sparkling smile. Rebecca put a comforting arm around his waist, "And unlike you they're celibate anyway."

"That's because they were either 'gay' or pregnant. Did you not know there was a Pope that was found to be pregnant?"

"Yes, I had heard of such. It must have been a surprise. Can I call you Lochy?"

"Yes, people do, but don't ever tell my Mother, she would be furious. She always called me Lochlan."

"My Ma and Pa hated Becky."

"What about yourself, how much do you know of your own family tree? The Stein's true Jew ancestry, all the way back to Moses?"

"Now you're being facetious. I know quite a bit. One of my ancestors was Gertrude Stein, you know, the one who was an early patron of Picasso. That's why I'm studying the creative period before the first world war, Fauvism, Cubism, Braque, Matisse, et al."

"Oh, the old et al," he said mockingly. "Now who is being obtuse? Gertrude must have been childless, unless Alice B Toklas, her life partner, was in drag and really a rose sporting a useful thorn, like Rose Salyvy. Marcel Duchamps alter ego."

"The artist who cross-dressed the Mona Lisa by adding a moustache?"

"Yes. That's the one."

"What are you saying?"

"She was a dyke, she liked women."

"Yes, I know, but most women may sometimes, you know."

"So, I've heard."

"She was childless of course, however, she was one of five children and I believe that we are related to her nephew Allan Stein. He knew Picasso as well and Matisse and promoted their infamous rivalry. His sister-in-law, Sarah, was for Matisse. My favourite incisive statement comes from Picasso to Matisse. *'You search for line, but have colour, and I search for colour, but have line'.* That's the basis of my comparison, my research and dissertation, at Berkeley."

"You don't say."

"Stop being so sarcastic and patronising with all your arty wit... Pro...fes...sor." The forceful emphasis she placed on her rendering of professor, surprised him. It was a thoughtful reminder that Rebecca was a feisty-women with her own agenda.

"Okay. Okay. Becky; I'm listening."

"Well. I have managed to trace our lineage way back to eighteenth century Russia, and as all marriages were within the Jewish faith, there were no unions with gentiles. It is a pure lineage through the female line; my Jewish allegiance is literally in my DNA."

"All marriages, yes, all marriages were between Jews, yes, but all unions? *Pure:* literally in your DNA? I think not," he said, interrupting.

"Who says so? You can't just say that," she said, incensed, as she felt he was treating her like a naïve student. "You have to qualify that statement Mr Pro…fes…sor."

"I'm just saying, when it comes to families, you can't always be truthful without alienating all, or some family members, especially in an autobiography, or even disguised in a novel, although many authors try. Listen; do you know of Kathleen Hale, the illustrator of the 'Orlando the Marmalade Cat' children's books in the 1920s?"

"No, not really, should I?"

"She was invited onto the BBC radio four's Desert Islands Discs a few years ago to mark her centenary. She told, Sue Lawley, the compare, she could now tell her own story as she wanted to set the record straight for her grandchildren and great grandchildren as she was now 100 years old and outlived her entire family. She wished to tell her story and not take it to the grave."

"What was so unusual about her story?"

"It's a true story. In her mid-twenties Kathleen Hale developed a tumour on her spine that affected her legs, and when she met the surgeon who was going to perform the operation for its removal, they both fell instantly and hopelessly in love, even though he was married with two sons and was a great deal older than her, more than twice her age I believe."

"Girls often want to marry their Dad, don't you know, there's is still hope for you."

"No way, marriage, not for me, not ever."

"Me too, but you may meet someone that's a game changer, we live in hope." Lochlan shrugged his shoulders in a gesture of contrition, and swiftly returned to his tale of Kathleen Hale.

"They had an affair, which had to be kept very secret. Because a divorce would have ruined a person's career. In the 1920s nobody got divorced."

"Honest."

"Yes, it was social taboo then. Consequently, to continue the affair and remain close to her lover, she married one of his sons."

"Really, that's way crazy; one of his sons?"

"Yes, she married his eldest son, only; incredibly; the father of both of her children was his father, his dad, the surgeon? And both families socialised and holidayed together, including the surgeon's wife. Kathleen continued to have a relationship with her lover and her husband, his son, and she insisted that nobody knew or suspected ever. Apparently, when Lawley asked her how she could be certain the father of her children was her lover's. She said, '*Come, come, Sue; we women have our ways of making sure of these things. I'm lucky as I have outlived all my relatives, but many an outrageous and unusual life story must be buried with the person and remain untold, especially if their revelation would have caused too much heart ache to loved ones; not to mention problems with their inheritance.*'

That's a true story. Few family lines are pure and without secrets. I believe I read somewhere, that a third of the people in central Europe, alive today, are descended from Genghis Khan."

"That accounts for your two world wars then."

"It doesn't really work like that."

"I know that, silly boy, I know that. But same faith marriages make it less open to controversy, although you can't know for certain. Why you could even be my father. Don't frown like that. Oh, come on, stop frowning. It was a joke and you're being all serious, I didn't mean that you look old, stop sulking. The Brethren are not asking you to be religious, it seems to me, they are asking you to be loyal to your roots: even if the lineage could be doubtful, as you say. Loyal, as I am, in my way, by undertaking my research, I feel a Jewish kinship."

"Well I don't, I don't feel anything. Any allegiance. I have values I guess, but no belief system, apart from a passion for academic rigour, honesty. I believe the truth should be told, so many wealthy and powerful people censor the truth, and rewrite history. *The truth is stranger than fiction* as they say and you know, really, it is. I bet if you *bone* up on your family tree, you will find a few skeletons. *Boom-Boom!*"

"Lochy. That's a terrible joke. But, well, yes, there is one 'skeleton' that implies that the large chunky nude women that Picasso painted between the wars, your wars..."

"They weren't my wars," Lochlan stressed, interrupting.

"Were based on Gertrude Stein and I do know what she meant, your Cat Lady; about waiting until people contemporary with the period are deceased to avoid controversy: I have a secret too, well our family has, but if you tell anyone, I will deny everything; everything: do you copy?"

"A.O.K, on pain of death, I'm Mr Stumm Majewski."

***

"Well, now: when I was still at school. We; me, my Pa and Ma, were staying on in Paris France for the summer."

"I love the way you Americans say Paris France as if it could be anywhere else."

"There is a place called Paris in Texas, that's why: and there is also a London and a Birmingham, and many more European place names, all over the US, that's maybe why we say where it is. Professor Lochlan." He felt belittled, as her tone intended.

"Anyway," she continued, "when we were in The Capital of France: Paris," she said this with a slow deliberate sarcasm, "my Dad took us to the Picasso National Museum. Apart from the permanent exhibits, they had a special exhibition of the photographs Picasso had taken throughout his life; he was no Bresson, but then he wasn't trying to be. These were studio working photos on 'glass plates', and 'negatives', that he had scratched into or drawn onto or on which flat areas of Indian ink had been added, to facilitate his imagination, I guess. Those on show were just a few hundred from the several hundred found by his executors. However, I remembered and never forgot what my Pa said to my Ma. *'It was a good thing that some of the nude photographs that Picasso took of Gertrude were not on display'* and then they laughed, but went on to say, *'that they had them at our home, and that they would be worth a fortune if they hadn't been censored by the family.'*

"Well I can certainly keep that little secret," he said dismissively.

"You bugger, you don't understand. I have seen the images. They are really rude, you know pornographic, rude."

"How rude?"

"Rude, rude; very rude, you know, hard core pornographic rude. She was a big stocky woman, and certainly was a right, or perhaps, sometimes, a left handful, in a few of them."

"Oh, I see."

33

"Well, there you go. The thing is a lot of the large, bulky women you see in Picasso's bathing and beach paintings were based on Gertrude, some of the nude photo's images actually prove this beyond doubt."

"That's a bit of a bombshell."

"You bet, your Kathleen Hale tale made me realise that's probably the reason I'm not allowed to refer to Gertrude and Picasso's affair in my dissertation."

"On pain of death?" he said mockingly.

"No, stop being silly Lochy; because many of her relations and extended family are still alive, as are his."

"I wonder what Toklas, her secretary and lifelong partner, would have had to say if she had known?"

"I'm not sure if she did know for certain, but it is also likely that she took many of the photos, although not proven, but she did try photography, mostly of food dishes, it was an interest of hers. Even Fernande, Piccaso's live-in love, may have been behind the camera. In 1906 Gertrude sat for over three months so Picasso could paint her portrait, visiting his studio every day, and the portrait still wasn't finished. What do you think one of the greatest artists with the most complete facility, arguably ever, was doing with his time?"

"Surely you should publish or be dammed, as they say. The press would have a field day, he is still a hot name, you would win a non-fiction award, and make your fortune."

"No such chance, as *they,* whomsoever *they* may be, in my extended family, but especially my uncle, said no chance. Too many vested interests I guess, but I will publish my research with photographs in the future, when *they* have all died, when it won't hurt anyone, like Kathleen Hale did."

"Well, you can't wait a lifetime to publish unless you are an optimist, as your family, The Stein Family, may have longevity in their genes. You may never publish. At this time, this decade, it would be a fascinating tome."

"I know. I was going to have Picasso's 'Les Demoiselles d' Avignon' as the cover image, you know, his famous brothel painting, juxtaposed with the photographic print on which he based the painting; as in a way a whore house is part of my teenage history. The woman crouching in the foreground is actually in a peeing position in the original photo."

"How apt! I must say. It's a brothel picture is it? I will view it differently from now on. I never saw it as an interior of a brothel image before. No wonder it's considered to be the forerunner of the drive towards the dead end offered by cubism. I would certainly piss on it."

"Hey, hold on there, big boy," Rebecca tried to interrupt, but Lochlan was in full flow.

"I can only say, if I was sitting on such controversial information, I would publish or be dammed. You have been censured; tempered by family values and opinion with no doubt some underlying deference to Jewish orthodoxy and not set store by the truth, I would publish as soon as you may, someone else may get hold of the negatives for a start. I wouldn't worry about causing the Family a loss of face, it's more important that truth and academic rigour must surely prevail."

"They won't be able to access any of them, because, according to my uncle, all of the photographic plates and negatives are in our family bank vault, including all the most compromising photographic prints. I don't know, really, your unusually honest and proper Lochy. Unlike most, self-opinionated, puffed up men who strut their stuff, and yet show no values, no loyalty, and no commitment to the truth."

"Well Becky, I do believe all aspects of research, academic, scientific, should be reported accurately and, of course, honestly. What else is there?"

"There are falsehoods, you know that. Much of art history has been rewritten and reinvented, mostly by men, to support the sale prices of established works of art, and at least a third of attributed artworks are known to be fakes anyway, the actual figure could be much higher. Artists cheat, they use photographs and you can always tell. Why it is evident to a practiced discerning eye that the triple or sometimes many more photographic exposures of the same subject, was Braque and Picasso's Cubist inspiration, although they kept that secret."

"Well, well, well, I never took you for an idealist Becky, you certainly are provocative and somewhat combative. I must say."

"What did you take me for then?

He smiled with a hint of mock self-pity before replying.

"Posh totty."

"What the hell is posh totty?" she said, raising her voice, apparently annoyed, although she knew what he implied, (and she liked it) unsure if she could follow through with her professional role while harbouring an undeniable attraction to her victim.

"Rich, well-educated, intelligent and beautiful... trailer trash."

She laughed, and making out to hit Lochlan, she pushed him back onto the large sofa-bed in the lounge, and had her way with him, amongst the cushions. Once she had placed her labia lips around his burgeoning erection, he was fucked, literally, as she rode him. He was late for his lecture and all in a rush. She shouted after him from the bedroom window as he ran out of the building entreating him to run, still laughing. She closed the window and went back to bed. Rebecca truly loved his smell when mingled with herself and breathed in down the neck of her makeshift night shirt and dozed. She was awoken by a female, about her own age, letting herself in to the apartment with her own key and calling out Lochy, Lochy. When she saw Rebecca standing in the bedroom doorway, she said sorry several times and bowing slightly, left whence she came, like a phantom. Rebecca was so light-headed from sleep and dreams that she had not said a word.

***

It was nearly time to phone her uncle, so after a shower and a very late breakfast Rebecca phoned.

"Yes, uncle, yes. We did access all the information you specified, yes. Confirming his ancestry, yes, and he seemed fairly convinced that he has an extended Jewish background and had an extensive Jewish family. He was well pleased that your *minions,* as he called them, had taken the trouble and intends to thank you. I let him have it on the loyalty angle as you suggested."

"Good girl."

"And he hasn't said that he was unable to undertake The Project, and seems committed to hearing from your team, and what it entails, and exactly how he is expected to fit in. He obviously realises it's to do with script translation and conservation from zero BC or there about, but also expects that it may require a little updating, those were his words. He has not mentioned Q and appears to have no intention of taking me into his confidence, but

36

he seems genuinely excited about something. And although I really hope it's me, I guess that it's your project."

"Splendid Rebecca, take a day, or should I say, a night off, and go and see your flatmate Rosemary. She has been asking after you incessantly the past few days. She knows she mustn't contact you, but perhaps you should keep your communication channels open and let her know when you may not be home sometimes. You may think you can take care of yourself, but she does not, and she worries; naturally."

"Oh, yes, that reminds me, our professor's cleaner let herself in, with her own key, she didn't clean, just left abruptly. Why wasn't I informed? She gave me quite a shock."

"Ah, dear me. Sorry Becky, we didn't know she had a key. She is not his cleaner, she comes some mornings, Thai girl, she's a hooker and waitress, married as well, but she may well clean for him. We thought it best not to tell you."

"Well that little shit. Fuck! I don't believe It. You have got to be fucking joking, uncle."

"Hey! hold on, it's just another assignment Rebecca, don't you get sweet on him young lady. He may have an appointment with his 'maker' in the next few days if he wants out and intends to go public, remember this Project is top priority."

"I'm just saying, you know: MEN."

"I know Becky my love, but we have to be non-judgemental, we have to remain detached. You have to remain detached, impartial. Is that clear?"

"Yes uncle: sorry, sorry."

"Okay. Now here's the deal. We have asked him to find his way, by public transport, to Saint Anne's, the church on the green at Kew, tomorrow. Do not go with him if he asks. Wait at his place for his return. Better not go out, as we will need to know his reaction to our proposition ASAP. Is that understood?"

"Yes of course."

"You may answer his phone calls and tell us if he gives you any information whatsoever which is to do with The Project, we would need to know immediately. You will not be asked to see him again if he declines. Under no circumstances should you agree to see him unless you have our say-so."

"Yes uncle."

**

Lochlan was walking the path to the church across Kew green. When he saw a car moving slowly in his direction. He just couldn't believe it, but it must be their car, he realised, on time. A black Mercedes with dark tinted windows, he smiled to himself. It pulled up and the driver got out and opened the rear door without saying a word. His height, build and persona allowed for no dissension. He oozed menace, in spite of the contradictory smell of his 'sweet' aftershave. It was so clichéd. Lochlan had the overwhelming impression he was in a B-movie and half expected to be told it was a hoax. He even suspected that he may have been set up by Summerskill, a faculty colleague, who, he was sure, attempted to undermine all his innovative teaching methods due to his, Lochlan's, enduring popularity with the students.

He fastened the seat belt in the back of the car as he was told and put on the totally opaque dark sun glasses the driver asked him to wear and plugged in the earphones which relayed the sound system. The music was loud. He could not see a thing or hear much exterior sound of the traffic, but later he assumed he was in central London from the starting and stopping and movement of the car. Eventually, after at least half an hour, he reasoned, the staccato rhythm of the traffic ended. Then the car waited for some time with its engine still running. He found the stop most unsettling, he had the sense of being in a dentist's chair, full of trepidation, yet numbed by the injection of the unrelenting rock beat. At least two Iron Maiden tracks Lochlan thought, and several Meatloaf. He hated Meatloaf, perhaps this was Summerskill's revenge. He knows I loathe this music. Then he felt the car move off, with caution over several road humps, then come to a stop.

As he was led away from the car and through a doorway, his nostrils were filled with the smell of ancient wood, damp masonry and second-hand bookshops. He loved that smell. He was still more than a little apprehensive, but was reassured somewhat, because from the outset he had assumed that a senior Rabbi such as Simon Cohen would be above any skulduggery.

"Good morning Professor Lochlan, come this way," a tall, fit, and muscle-bound doorman said as he started frisking him with an electronic device, after removing the earphones, music system and shades. He was also asked to put his keys, mobile phone and watch in a draw and take off his shoes (which were inspected and returned) before being sent along a dark corridor to the end door. He was beginning to find the whole situation ridiculous, especially his recent frisking. As he walked Lochlan was anxiously contemplating doing a runner. He had changed his mind about the whole nefarious set up, and wanted out, but the overlarge doorman was blocking his retreat.

***

At the opening door and blinking against the light he strained to define the profile that presented itself on the other side. It was Rabbi Simon Cohen.

"Come in, Professor Majewski, do sit down and have some tea, several sorts over there, or café, double espresso I believe, a bit early for something stronger, I think, don't you?"

The room was not in any way anonymous, he had expected a bland office with no reference points, nothing memorable or traceable, but this was a grand back room of a palace or maybe the lounge of an exotic town house. The plasterwork on the high ceiling was intricate and part gilded. Crystal chandeliers hung from several ornate bosses. Elegant cartouches enriched the walls. On the oak parquet floor was an extremely large chinoiserie carpet, as soft as sand underfoot. The seating was arranged around a low rectangular table with leather chesterfield sofas on both sides, and matching arm chairs at either end. Lochlan soon realised the vast hall widows were set too high for anyone to take in an exterior view, even if they jumped or stood on a chair. The Brethren have considered every detail of the venue, and it was too elaborate to be a hoax: maybe, just maybe, this is for real, he considered. He was circumspect, but excited.

Seated were four men in well-tailored suits, who stood up in choreographed unity for a formal introduction. They looked like slick lawyers, to Lochlan. Who wasn't expecting to see God fearing men, robed in purple and gold, but he was anticipating some religious reference in their attire, a white clerical 'dog collar,' perhaps? This took him by surprise, as it alluded to the possibility that this was clandestine, and secret, and their indirect threats on his future, (or lack of it) were for real. He was a bit concerned.

As he was being introduced, he was grinning, stifling the giggles, something he was prone to when tense, but also because the situation was so surreal. He was introduced to Bishop Frankford, the Archbishop of Canterbury's Representative and the other two, were introduced as Cardinal Lopez the Chief representative of the Catholic church in Europe and Bishop Jenkins, (of whom he registered some dim knowledge or recognition of the voice), the Anglican Church leader in Wales. He was surprised to see a member of the Greek Orthodox church who was introduced as Bishop Sotakos, an authority on early Christian manuscripts. Lochlan was acquainted with his work. After shaking hands and exchanging pleasantry's, he sank nervously into a seat. He still had the feeling that he was in a film, but he also realised that stupidly, he hadn't taken the precaution of telling anyone about this little outing: no one knew where he was and nor did he. He was determined to find out.

***

"We are sorry you were subjected to our airport style security downstairs, Professor, but we are all subject to it here. It's just precautionary," Archbishop Frankford said.

"Yes, it did seem a tad excessive, especially the clandestine journey here, where are we exactly?" he did not elicit an answer.

"We meet once a month on the full moon Professor, when we are able, and rotate the chair annually. I am our present chair. It is unusual to get us all together at the same time, in person, as we use internet conferencing for absentees, but this is a special project as you have been made aware. How do you feel about all this Professor Majewski?"

"Well I feel awestruck to be truthful and most uncomfortable, I seem to be amongst an auspicious Christian brotherhood."

"Quite so, very good, indeed you are. You are here under difficult circumstances, but if we take this further all the security procedures will make sense. Do you have any questions before we begin? We may as well get straight down to business, don't you think?"

"Yes, that's okay by me, but I do have one overriding concern."

"Go ahead."

"How come you chose me for this your Q Project. There are several renowned ecclesiastical researchers and conservationists, Debra Morrison at Michigan, Barrymore at the Sorbonne, and others who have championed the possibility of Q. Aren't there?"

"Yes, yes, indeed, they were all well researched by Sotakos, were they not?" The Bishop nodded. "We considered you to be the most eminent candidate, quite honestly, and they also have extensive family commitments we believe." Sotakos nodded again.

"And I'm single, without responsibilities, was that a factor?"

"It *is* a factor, yes, Professor, an overriding factor. This is a secret project, it cannot and will not be compromised."

"Well, well, that gets straight to the nub of my anxieties and answers many of my other queries. You have been most kind to invite me, but, okay, now I know where I stand. Clearly. The Rabbi," Lochlan gestured towards Rabbi Cohen, "has made sure that not a single communication between us has been written down or recorded, not one and no one knows I'm here and I don't even know where we are. You seem to have all the cards Brethren. So, tell me, *what is it that I have to do for you?*" While he waited for an answer, he heard the clock of Big Ben striking the hour, ten gongs, close bye, he thought.

***

Bishop Frankford asked the Bishop Sotakos to start, and he described the stacks of clay tablets that were found packed in cases at Lord Soane's House, in London, at Lincoln Inn Fields.

"Each tablet had been inscribed individually, but the tablets had been fused, by age and humidity into numerous blocks as the tablets had originally been air dried after their surface was incised, not kiln fired. They had been discovered in a dry culvert, an ancient Roman cistern in Jordan, during excavations in 1825 and bought in a job lot by Lord Soane's, an itinerant and compulsive British collector. His addiction had been our good fortune, because he was a hoarder and threw nothing away. The clay tablets were inscribed with administrative records and were

41

dated using the Julian Calendar, but the Gregorian dates equate to a period 10 BC to 20 AD. They had been overlooked until recently as only the tops of the blocks of tablets were discernible. Each tablet was the same size, approximately 15 cm square. Attempts by Soane's and others to separate them were futile. However, a decade ago, when the relatively new scanning techniques of X-Ray Computed Tomography were applied to the blocks, the scanners were able to separate, at least visually, each layer, and 'read' the majority of the tablet's inscriptions. Most of the inscriptions were the tedious records of the day to day running of an empire, of considerable interest to sociologists and historians, but our interest was focused on the inscriptions that contained information that related to the logia teachings and quotations from Jesus of Nazareth."

"So, you *have* found Q," Lochlan said excitedly. "It seems like you have, that's so cool?" He was beginning to understand the enormous consequences of the potential dissemination of the tablet's contents, to 'the media', feeling quite emotional as he realised, that this was for real. After his enthusiastic outburst, he looked towards Rabbi Cohen and caught his 'on pain of death' look. Which was the actor's disapproval of Lochlan's, *that's so cool.*

"Which may have also included," the bishop continued, while not appreciating the interruption, "the actual tablets that could have been distributed by his followers. As the content from several of these tablets were in duplicate, we believe this points to the possibility. Several of the tablets refer to information that may have been supplied by 'Roman' agents who were active within Judea at the time."

"Really! Jesus!" Lochlan shouted. "Sorry... I meant... really Jesus," he then said quietly, curtailing his enthusiasm. They all chuckled at this, including Lochlan.

"Now Professor, every biblical researcher will know, Q is a hypothetical source for the Gospel of Matthew and of Luke, as there is common material found in the Gospel of Matthew and Luke, but not in the Gospel of Mark. Certain anomalies in their writing of all three Gospels and others have led scholars, eminent scholars, such as yourself Professor, to differing and contentious views. You have always maintained the view that JC's teachings and sayings must have been written down originally, have you not? Even if destroyed by time, or by the authorities."

"Yes, it does seem totally logical to me. One or more of JC's… can I say JC's…?" his audience all nodded their approval in unison. "Okay, okay, one or more of JC's entourage must have produced a flyer or something that acknowledged that he was *on the road* and *coming to a town near you.* Surely some of his speeches, sayings, descriptions of miracles, something written in some form, would precede and accompany his journeys, even though we assume that most of the apostles and his followers were illiterate. Not all were and of course the literate, the scribes, as you well know, made a good living from writing and reading for and to the illiterate." Lochlan had almost forgotten why he was there and was beginning to treat the whole discussion like an academic seminar or conference. The earlier trepidation and concerns of his impending demise, almost forgotten.

"I have never been so sure Professor," Bishop Frankford said. "I have tended to side with Karl Lachman's well-argued proposition that the Gospel of Mark was the first of the three Synoptic Gospels. While others subscribe to the Farrer Hypothesis, which still puts the Gospel of Mark as an original source of course. However, it seems I have been wrong, and the recent readings have shown us that JC's preachings could have been set down on these small clay tablets, then finally sun dried. The process would have rendered the script to be clear, but inevitably fragile. This would be a cheap process, with JC's thoughts, teachings, and ideas handed out like propaganda leaflets. They could be handled carefully and even stored for a few years, but eventually most of them would have deteriorated." Bishop Frankford took a few deep breaths, another sip of water, and continued.

"We are very lucky to possess the few we have Professor. Bishop Sotakos was asked to catalogue and translate all the tablets from the Romano/Greek. This took him and his assistants over two years as the tablets contained references to the day to day administration of Judea by Rome or officials appointed via Rome. During this arduous process he managed to see the importance of the dates in the reports from Palestine Judea and secreted the relevant scanner images immediately."

"Well done Bishop, I'm sure I would have done much the same if I had been privy to their content. Any leak of the discovery would have blown the lid off their true interpretation."

"Yes, quite so Professor," Bishop Frankford said after Lochlan's unwelcome intrusion to a script he had been memorising for several days, and continued. "He gave a synopsis of their content to his Archbishop, who immediately saw their importance and took steps to introduce Bishop Sotakos to the Christian Brotherhood. Years of discussion have now brought us to this point."

The Bishop then gave out a full text translation to everyone, presented in a loose leaf spiral bound folder, which also included an image of the appropriate tablet from which the text was translated. Lochlan who agreed with most of Sotakos's translation, argued more about the exact meaning of some words in context. They all laughed however when Lochlan said, "It was just like reading through JC's time line."

Several graphics including a horizontal chart, allowed them to see more clearly the sequence of the recorded events and the corresponding dates. A map of *The Holy Land* showed them the position of the various towns, or locations with their modern names, where relevant, to cross reference. Professor Lochlan didn't wait to be asked for his opinion again, he was just so excited at what he was reading. Eventually he couldn't contain his enthusiasm.

"Oh! My God! This is just so incredible, isn't it! this seems to be irrefutable proof that an agent was providing information to the Roman command in their Province of Judea and that he was a paid informant and was, to all intents and purposes a local agent. He may have even been a false apostle who deliberately infiltrated JC's crowd. How many people are aware of these tablets, this information?" he asked.

"The recently separated information is known world-wide academically. You may well remember the original tablets findings from the I.C.E. although you would have been quite young Professor. Their content was widely reported, apart that is, from the ones that you have before you. The only persons aware of their content are in this room. Apart from one other, a VIP, a dignitary. Someone who you will certainly meet later if we make progress."

"They should be published pronto, don't you think? I feel as if my life has been on hold, just waiting for this. And who's the dignitary? I am most intrigued."

"Well maybe; we do intend to publish," Lopez said, deliberately avoiding answering Lochlan's secondary question. "As you can see all the tablets are dated, and some are quite possibly the very first truly centrally administered state police records, and much of the content the actual translation of JC's words."

"Wow," Lochlan exclaimed. "We have to remember, the most recent reporting of JC's Ministry we had prior to this discovery, was The Codex Leviticus, as you will all know." Lochlan's intonation rose towards the end of this sentence to imply a question, without asking one. Rabbi Cohen (The actor Paul Smith), sighed his disapproval at this tendency of the young. "The oldest New Testament in the world, which is mostly written in 350 A D from disparate information set down 100 A D approximately, including The Four Apostle's. That's 100 years after JC's death. They are so important, and the peoples of the World should know about this, they really should, and pronto," he emphasised. "Why have you sat on this for so long. Why? For heaven's sake."

"I think you had better take responsibility for that answer, Cardinal." Bishop Frankford gave Lopez his cue to take part in the proceedings.

"Yes, of course, Frank." Cardinal Lopez stood up to talk, but took a few seconds before beginning, as Bishop Frankfort had glared at Cardinal Lopez for his lapse into familiarity. This was not noticed by Lochlan who was so absorbed in the subject.

"The late Pope, God rest his soul," he genuflected, "was absolutely insistent that the information on the Q-gate Tablets, that is how he always referred to them, didn't he?" he said this while looking around at his colleagues, Lochlan noticed all the Brethren nodded in agreement, "should be released truthfully and unabridged. Not selectively as he believed was the case with the Dead Sea Scrolls. He was adamant, putting preventative measures in place to foil any release of information regarding the Q Tablets. However; the current Pope has been less intransigent, more proactive and even directly involved. The recent Pope, but not our present father, was the Cardinal *Rat*, who decided to sit on it. There are those who believe that he may have been saving

45

the publication of the Q tablets until he had engineered his own Reign, but I am unqualified to say. He certainly gave the green light during his tenure."

"I see, yes, the release of the Texts will ennoble any Pope's period in office for all time. Now I see. I am beginning to realise exactly why I am here undercover."

"Let's have lunch and we will try to explain our position, Professor."

***

The Christian Brothers led the way into the dining room next door. The windows were to one wall, glazed with stained glass far too dense, Lochlan noticed, to see outside. A comprehensive buffet lunch had been spread on a large oak table. The food was all *meet, eat and greet* and most conducive to conversation. Rabbi Cohen would have made sure of this Lochlan noted. Professor Lochlan Majewski still felt like he was in a film, as if the various parties were working from a script, but the Q tablets and their translation had really gelled his enthusiasm. He really felt that he was just so fortunate to be part of something so exciting and potentially momentous and was so pleased that he had been asked; yet he still had the disconcerting sense that something wasn't quite right.

Lochlan didn't really mind what perceived use may be made of The Project in the future, for he understood that the final translation, (no matter how it may be presented, even if disseminated honestly with considerable respect for the truth) would be misrepresented and misconstrued to further whatsoever bias a group or individual held. Of this he was certain as this was the case with any presentation of academic research, religious or otherwise of which he was aware. Even his own published work on the 'Tapa prints' of Fiji and Samoa had been used to endorse and promote the various groups seeking the independence of these South Sea Islands.

Still feeling as if he was at school, Lochlan instinctively asked Bishop Frankford if he could leave the room to visit the toilet. There were several, giving him a choice of 6 cubicles and as many individual urinals. He was surprised at the number. This must be a club or lodge building of some kind, he thought. He stood on a toilet seat in one of the cubicles and peered through the crack in an opaque window through which he was able to make out a small van that had Kew Cuisine writ large on its side with the slogan *Gourmet meals delivered to your door,* written underneath. He sat down again and was just wondering why anyone should order mobile catering from Kew, an area a long way from central London, when he heard the main lavatory door open and the voice of Cardinal Lopez asking if he was alright. Lochlan pulled the flush and joined the Brethren in the main hall.

Lochlan was beginning to question the whole set up. It seemed too good to be true. What was it his mum had said; *if something seems too good to be true then it is probably not true.* He had missed out on several occasions by not believing the hype. Wendy for a start: when he was only fifteen, and she turned out to be *a real goer* as the boys said. He was the only one in the 5 aside football team to still be a virgin at the end of the season. When she told the team, she didn't mind *five aside,* she meant it. He thought of his Mum's dictum and went home. Wendy settled for *four aside.*

***

Then Bishop Frankfort, took the opportunity to explain. "How the Christian Brotherhood formed after the fall of the Shah of Iran in 1979 when the Islamic fundamentalists had taken power led by Ayatollah Khomeini. The Shah, although, not a Christian, was seen to be pro-Western. His deposition was a wake-up call to all Christians. In Beirut, at the same time, the Muslims and the Christians were going head to head and dying in thousands during the Lebanese Civil War.

It was, therefore, decided, during protracted exchanges between differing Christian religions, to form a Christian Brotherhood of disparate religious doctrines, who were united in their dedication to the sustenance and promotion of The Christian Ministry. This was a decisive turning point, historically; the first time that separate Christian religious sects or beliefs had united behind a common purpose. The Brotherhood had continued to meet monthly to promote Christ's Ministry by all and every means at their disposal. Hence their motto. *Per Omnes et omnis medium. (By All and Every Means.)*"

Professor Lochlan Majewski swallowed nervously and took note.

Bishop Frankfort went on to say, "Their cause had not been assisted by the Middle Eastern and Afghan wars and the general Christian malaise within western society, but they now believed this contemporary account by local informers, including a JI who may well have been Judas Iscariot, could have the potential to galvanise non-believers and followers of Christ's doctrine in an unprecedented way."

"Do you really think so? Judas could have been a Roman Agent?" Lochlan asked, addressing all the Brethren.

"We're being speculative now, we can do that later," Bishop Frankfort said. "So, that's The Project, to assimilate the knowledge and present the contemporary record in a tangible form."

***

Rabbi Cohen asked Lochlan to step out into the courtyard, while the Christian Brothers considered how to proceed. He gave him 'The Proposal' to read while they deliberated. He was pleased to be outside. Pushing up his sleeve, he automatically looked for his absent watch: they had been in the hall for at least 3 hours he had judged from Big Ben's chime's. We must be central he concluded, he could smell the river as he watched a blackbird pick the moss off the cloisters stone tiles, seeking grubs. He was sure that the whole building had been or maybe still was a Bishops palace. 17th maybe 18th century. He could see no easy method of escape from the courtyard, especially as he had no head for heights and never understood the desire of anyone to climb up anything.

He sat down and started to read a synopsis, that he had been given, it was an un-signed A 4 print. He recognised that it was in one sense a manifesto, but it could not be used as proof if he informed anyone of the meeting. He was also aware it was meant to keep him occupied while the Brethren debated his appointment. A procedure that he often used with prospective students. It was a device to reduce their nervousness, while their future was decided.

The Proposal

We believe it is the time for a new cathedral, of exceptional grandeur, to be built in Europe. There is an urgent need as the Islamic religions are establishing new and larger places of worship at an alarming rate. This is excellent for the integration of our immigrant populations and multiculturalism, but it may be anathema to the established Christian church in Europe and the West in general.

There are many corporations who would subscribe to a fund set up for the building of a great Christian Cathedral and many established architectural practices who will offer their services for free, such is the prestige. It is generally agreed by most political parties and all ecumenical divisions of Christianity that there is a great need for this strong statement of our faith. However, wealthy corporations and individuals will not sign up until there is agreement on the capital city in which the new cathedral should be built, or, indeed, the denomination. There is so much dissent, even the chosen few of our Brotherhood cannot decide. This has gone on for two decades.

Also, as you may well imagine, individuals are polarised between the traditional grand modern, similar to Gaudi's Sagrada Familia in Barcelona, or ultra-modern using new and innovative building technique's aka 'Gherkins' and 'Shards'. There are as many opinions as there are vested interests. However, and this is the crux of the matter, if the cathedral could be financed by the public, by public subscription, this would make the cathedral decision, much easier.

We believe that the translation of the Tablets into the more presentable form of a book (that was the proven and verified contemporary account of Jesus Christ's Ministry) would be a world best seller of the like never before seen. The sum of money raised would be substantial and in the absence of an agreement, (by the various party's) on the location, it would leave the way open for the Capital City to be selected by chance. Names of a possible location taken from a hat so to speak. To this end we encourage you to further this development.

As Lochlan read this, he noticed that certain phrases or grammar gave away the author... *best seller like never before seen,* and not... *like never seen before. Or...so to speak.* It still wasn't proof that it was penned by Rabbi Cohen either. When Lochlan challenged his students, (if he considered some written piece to be plagiarism) for deviation from their normal sentence construction and grammar; he was suspicious, but it wasn't proof.

Lochlan was also aware of the vast income potential the publication of Q could generate and understood his own payment would be a minuscule percentage of the revenues. He was also of the opinion that there probably was, and quite possibly will be, considerable bickering amongst the various factions of the Christian leadership, and he was not so naïve as to assume all 'the monies' would go towards church or cathedral construction as he assumed, (as has been endemic throughout ecclesiastical history) vast sums would be subsumed by the administrative hierarchy to their own ends.

***

"Brothers, as Chair, I think the time has come to offer The Project to Professor Lochlan: are we all happy for Professor Lochlan Majewski to know The Project in its entirety. Do retract now Brothers as he is still able to leave with the knowledge we have imparted so far. His story will not be believed, his only contact is you Paul and you have obviously been most convincing. All our alibis are in place and he has no clue where we are or who we really are. He only knows who we say we are. He is our man I think."

"We also have a certain urgency, Brothers," Sotakos said. "We don't believe that Turkey will settle the Armenian genocide question any time soon, however, but they may, and if not, they are still networking and lobbying overtime to enter the European community, and currying favour by managing and entrapping, the refugee bulge on its borders. A Kudish genocide may even be on the cards. So, we must try to take this opportunity to further the pre-eminence of our doctrine and beliefs in Europe. However, our Professor may not want to work as solitary as we will require to keep this secret."

"Quite so Abe," said Bishop Frankford, using Bishop Abel Sotakos's nickname. "We are all committed to the reunification of Cyprus, via its re-Christianisation and I personally believe Nicosia should be our first option for an astonishing new Christian Centre and Cathedral to facilitate that possibility, as you all know. I also believe that Paul may have found our Professor a willing and trustworthy female assistant. Are we all in favour of asking Professor Lochlan to proceed?" Bishop Frankford asked. "I know his Dean and his head of faculty so we could set the ball rolling within weeks." All mumbled or nodded their agreement. "Well let's go outside and join him, I rather fancy some sunshine. You may now answer any of his questions truthfully if he commits."

Lochlan was seated at a long wooden table, when The Brethren filed out of the hall and came towards him. They looked much smaller outside, and older, he thought. He tried not to stare, but he had noticed that Cardinal Lopez was smoking a panatela, the smoke still smelt desirable, even though he had broken the habit himself, several years ago. I guess I am more tense than I realise, he thought and chastised himself.

"We have come to join you in the sun," Bishop Frankford said. And they all seated themselves around his table. The Cardinal sat directly opposite and Lochlan spoke to him so he could breathe in his smoke. The Cardinal was of stocky build, with dark cold eyes, set in a large shaven head which was divided by a pronounced beak of a nose. This was framed by unruly eyebrows and over large ears. He was in his mid-fifties and rocked rhythmically as he walked spreading his short fledgling arms slightly. Lochlan wondered if the Cardinal was going to be his minder.

"This is a lovely spot you have here," Lochlan remarked. "Is this your H.Q?"

"No, no, we meet at a different establishment and country each month, although we have been here a few times. Just a precaution. You have a splendid room next to mine, I will show you later."

"Now," Bishop Frankford said decisively. "You're in the picture and we have all agreed that you're the man to take The Project forward. The remuneration will be considerable, and the accolades far reaching, as you know. From what you have assimilated so far, are you willing, Professor?"

Lochlan had thought of nothing else for the past few days, but The Brethren's Project. He was flattered that he had been asked to decipher and promote Q to the world. He also believed, in some way, it was his calling, as he felt exonerated for his PhD thesis that pre-empted the discovery of Q. He had thought about loyalty, as Rebecca had countenanced. Loyalty to his grandmother's memory and his mother's faith and how he didn't really give much thought to his Jewish origins.

His interest in religious manuscripts was mostly chance. His main interest was in the conservation of ancient written material as he was charmed by the sheer breath-taking beauty of many calligraphic scripts and embellishments. He was encouraged to undertake The Project, because he dared himself to change his life and he was sure, in some way it would be life changing. Yes, he thought, 'I have worked very hard to achieve what I have, very hard, and the remuneration has been pitiful even for a single man in Central London, well Hackney, but even so'. He had given some consideration to the money as it would enable him to undertake self-initiated projects of his own; although he would have undertaken The Project for his present annual income, as in truth, he hated teaching nowadays, well lecturing. Mentoring his carefree students while they were taking up his suggestions and developing them within their own studies; when they were often ideas he wanted to develop for himself.

Lochlan also felt, the whole educational ethos had changed in the past few years, as he believed that everything was prescribed and so PC. Especially when considering student staff liaisons. Although, he was clearly aware, that if his students had been less mature, he might well have been paraded on Saville Row. In his opinion, when he first started lecturing, there was a much more friendly atmosphere in the faculty, more familiarity, sarcasm, ridicule and banter between student and lecturer and it seemed natural, par for the course, but no longer. In fact, he believed that he spent more time now on administrative dribble than lectures. He thrilled at the idea of financial security, but he was also apprehensive about the clandestine nature of the whole business. He knew there would *not* be a written contract; that he would have only *their* word, but, he surmised, 'if you cannot rely on the word of five ecclesiastical heavyweights, who can you trust'? It may seem too good to be true, but he was a gambler after all and having weighed up the odds, he had made up his mind.

"I will do your Project," he announced.

"Splendid, splendid dear boy, splendid," Bishop Frankford said immediately, and shook his hand. He seemed genuinely pleased and the brethren clapped enthusiastically. Lochlan couldn't help feeling, Rabbi Cohen was receiving the applause, as he detected a thwarted bow.

"We will go back into the hall and bring you up to speed," said Cohen with obvious delight.

"Wonderful, splendid," Bishop Frankford said again, placing his hand on Lochlan's shoulder as they walked towards the doorway.

Professor Lochlan Majewski was still not sure if it was necessarily a hand of God.

***

"Congratulations everyone," said Bishop Frankford. "I believe that we can now make rapid progress. As you are aware Professor Lochlan, an extremely influential V I P conceived and initiated the idea of a contemporary account of JC's ministry, travels, death, that could be verified by the release of the relevant Q tablets. Bishop Sotakos, has done his best to translate the colloquialisms and the language of the period, but we require your additional incite and expertise and authoritative confirmation of authenticity. We were going to release this brief, but contemporary account as a small book, and on all E platforms. A translation if you like of the factual elements of some of the Q tablets, but a modern translation none the less. You would be working with the Bishop Lochlan."

"How long do you think you will need my services?"

"That very much depends on your commitment, your work rate, but my guestimate would be 200 to 300 hours as the actual import of your translation will have to be agreed by all. It would take considerably less time, of course, if you had a trustworthy competent assistant."

"Okay. I understand my role and I certainly comprehend the need for secrecy. When do I start and when do we hope to publish?"

"As soon as is possible."

"Great, I can't wait to get started," Lochlan enthused.

They all looked from one to the other in amazement. The realisation that all their deliberations and planning may come to fruition, suddenly dawned on the Brethren, and they were overcome.

"Thank you," said an embarrassed Lochlan. "I am off to my room, this has been a tiring and yet exciting day, both the delicious food and the food for thought has been marvellous, and I thank you all and your invisible staff."

Cardinal Lopez left with him and showed, or some would say, escorted Lochlan to his room. Lochlan showered and was ready for bed and although it was early evening, the wine and above all his anxiety, had exhausted him. He puffed up the pillows against the heavy mahogany head board, slipped under the covers, and was soon asleep.

***

Lochlan was last down to breakfast, most had eaten and were on their coffee, Sotakos was outside for the first smoke of the day. They were all still smartly dressed, although casual, he noted. He felt dishevelled, physically and mentally. He had slept badly. Just too many *ifs* and *buts* swirling through his mind. Even his bedroom and the staircase windows overlooked the courtyard, several solid doors he tried to open were locked securely, and he still had no idea of the building's location. From the considerable morning chorus, (that included a grumpy cacophony from a rookery, and the general argumentative chatter of jackdaws) he assumed that there was probably a London park nearby, although, he was unable to discern any persistent traffic hum which was often punctuated by the sirens of emergency vehicles. He could, however, still hear at times, the faint chimes of Big Ben. He was puzzled to say the least.

He poured himself a coffee and drank it just as it came. Bishop Jenkins greeted him and seemingly in a hurry, started the conversation.

"Let's get the remuneration out of the way shall we Professor?" Lochlan sort of sighed his approval.

"We will give you a Pearl Card, like this one." Bishop Jenkins (who was obviously the Brotherhood's finance director as he had previously said very little) held up a credit card which had the simulated appearance of mother of pearl. "Only members of the Brotherhood have this card. This card can be used internationally and can be used to withdraw any amount of cash, when and if needed, and pay for meals, transport, flights, taxis, trains, that sort of thing. You will get a draw down facility for life, you may continue to use your Pearl Card for day to day use, hotels taxis etc. You will have this operational immediately, up to a single daily purchase of 2,000 $ U. S. You will also receive a sum of 20,000,000 $ US to be deposited with a broker on completion, but this will come to you as a legacy and in the form of shares."

"Well now, thanks for that, I think we can do business. It is a considerable sum. You must realise that I am enamoured with The Project, and I would love the money, and if that was an official legally binding contract I would be as far 'over the moon' as any Premier League footballer, but I shall just have to take your word for that *Contract,* as I have to, don't I?"

"And we will have to take your word, Professor. That you will undertake the work and keep your vow of absolute silence. Your silence commands a price that is equitable with that which you may receive for your knowledge of Q's existence."

The latter was said by Bishop Frankford and everyone stood up and shook Lochlan's hand in turn while he remained seated. Professor Lochlan Majewski knew the handshakes were contractual, *on pain of death*, regarding his secrecy. And there was absolutely no way out.

***

Rebecca had been waiting anxiously for a report from her uncle, the actor, Paul Smith. She knew that he had been rehearsing the oral responses and pious actions, that would be tested during Lochlan's induction weekend. Her uncle had told her he was troubled that Professor Lochlan would not be convinced. She was also doubtful and assumed her Lochy wouldn't want to be involved, but she was saddened, as his refusal would mean she would have to move on and move out of his life. She realised, much to her surprise; she had grown quite fond of him.

"Hello Becky."

"Oh! Hi. Go on tell me the worst uncle."

"No, it's all good. He went for it, all signed and sealed as it were. We are on our way."

"No, really? That's so disappointing. I somehow thought he was a straight guy. Well. That's me done then?"

"As a matter of fact, it isn't, he wants you as his assistant, although he doesn't know it yet. Is that alright with you? Collating, printing that sort of thing, secretarial. We need you to keep an eye on him. Bishop Jenkins thinks he might renege. We need you close, but not *too* close, is that possible Rebecca."

"Great, sounds good to me. How long will you need me?"

"Two months, maybe more, if not long hours."

"What about my studies, I am interested in continuing."

"I knew you would be Becky, I have arranged a term's deferment, if that's not too disruptive."

"Fine by me, as I guess it will have to be, but I'm a bit troubled about telling Rose as we were going to start the term together."

***

Soon everything was GO. Lochlan's sabbatical arranged via his superiors without his intervention. Filing cabinets delivered to his apartment, with the relevant Tablets facsimiles on memory sticks and hard copy and catalogued. Even new crisp laptops with enhanced memory and his assistant appointed, because; when Lochlan was asked if he knew an intelligent, able person who could help with the work in a secretarial capacity, he was well pleased when Becky said yes immediately. He assumed The Brothers would be sceptical, but he convinced them that Rebecca would believe he was undertaking his usual research and development for his next academic publication. Perhaps she remembered what he had said to her in the café; that the work was well paid, he thought cynically.

He was excited about the work, but a bit miffed that his name would not go down in history, comprehensively attached to Q, as every academic wants to find their 'Grail', but he understood why his name would only be credited for the authentication. Bishop Sotakos would of course be credited with its discovery and translation. Hey, ho, but he was going to be rich. He took the Pearl card from his wallet and kissed it.

***

Lochlan and Rebecca worked well together. She had moved in under the pink duvet, having established that his cleaner of the past four years was an ex-hooker, and thus retained. Also, in terms of the deadline for The Project, it was a more efficient arrangement. There was no underground to Hackney and the taxi from Marylebone was frequently delayed. She was always up earlier than he as she felt slightly nauseous in the mornings, and he was quite bright late evening when, armed with his Pearl Card, they nearly always went out to eat. Thai, Vietnamese, Sushi, Canton, Malay, and Sunday lunch at the Inn On The Park. Lochlan had always tried to keep Sunday a non-working day, nothing to do with acknowledging the Sabbath, but more to do with release and renewal.

He found academic writing tedious, although he acknowledged the research could at times be exciting. Often the detective work unfolded and revealed as some cryptic clues may in a crossword, but the Brethren's Q project was more straight forward and lacked the thrill of research and detection. The momentous prize of being involved in one of the greatest Christian discoveries was compensation of course and working with a beautiful assistant helped. Rebecca proved to be an accomplished organiser and exhibited an informed, sharp intelligence, he was not only beginning to recognise, but enjoy.

They had been to the Cautauld Institute, (Somerset House) Rebecca's place of study, to view the Post Impressionists paintings of the permanent collection, and he was most impressed by her conversation. When fatigued, more than once, by the necessarily slow viewing pace, they took time out in The Gallery Café. Their conversation concerned aspects of the exhibition's artworks.

Rebecca's proposition to Lochlan was that Westerners, communicating via Latin script, (i.e. most European languages) 'read' all images, paintings etcetera, in much the same way as they read writing. Left to right, instinctively. Even when outdoors or on entering a room. Westerner's, she believed, scan images, from the top left, of an image, to bottom right; scanning side to side across the image, downwards. The Chinese read from the bottom right, up and down an image, moving their eyes to the left up and down, ending up in the top left corner. Its' similar for the Japanese, she suggested, only from the left to right. The same way they 'read' their written work, or when a tutor calls for names as a 'register' in front of a class of students. Moving their eyes as if reading a page. This meant, she concluded, that the space depicted in a Japanese print, or ceramics, Chinese scroll or print would make sense to literate Chinese or Japanese, who would scan the image in the same manner that the Chinese or Japanese artists would have read a page of writing, but that it would look flattened to *Westerners,* when scanning intuitively from top to bottom, left to right.

At the turn of the Nineteenth century, Monet and Van Gogh possessed hundreds of Japanese prints, she explained, but they considered them to be a depiction that flattened space. Not dissimilar she concluded, to the flattening of the space that was apparent in the then, recent, advent of photography and therefore evident in late impressionist and post-impressionist painting. Rebecca also made out a good case for the monochrome, black and white daguerreotype and early photography having forced the Impressionists and later the Fauves to abandon evident chiaroscuro and emphasize the two things that early photography was unable to emulate; the spontaneity (i.e. an impression) and colour. He began to 'like the cut of her jib' as his Dad would say, as on their return to the galleries, he was able to view many of the paintings differently. Partly due to a meeting of minds, and possibly because, having lusted initially, slowly and imperceptibly, mocking all common sense and education, he was falling in love. A love that stealthily rewires the brain, ignoring the curlew's plaintive cry across the marshy quagmires as the incoming tide sweats in its salty brine.

Rebecca's feelings for Lochlan were consummated, however, on their first night together. Tempered by her deceitfulness, of course, yet still responding to his considerate lovemaking. Ney, as skilful as the playing of an end blown flute

**

They had been to the races at Newbury, Sandown, and recently Ascot, and although Rebecca had seen Trotting races in Paris and Deauville, this was her initiation to thoroughbred racing on the flat. She loved being at the races. Her flatmate, Rosey, went with them to Ascot and it was just as well as Lochlan became focused on the racing, or should that be betting, and mostly ignored them. He spent ages studying the form and looking for *value,* as he called it, while downing beer. He had never had such a big wager, but the money roll was much smaller at the end of the day than he had hoped, having just missed one that came in at big odds by a whisker. Well by three lengths to be precise. He said that he had *a pony* riding on it which confused the girls.

The girls had a great time, laughing and flirting with all and sundry. They did look young and gorgeous as they had chosen their clothes well and Rebecca won a free bet with the Tote for being judged to be one of the best turned out Ladies. She was a little surprised to find out later the best turned out horses were also judged. Lochlan said, 'It was probably the same team that judged both,' so she whacked him with her programme.

The girls bet on a horse when they liked the name, or if they fancied the look of the horse or groom, or both. They only bet to win, unlike Lochlan who did various permutations; and although they always lost, they had one win which gave them most of their money back and they couldn't contain their joy as their horse came past them as they stood at the rails, well out in front. Just beating a horse on which Lochlan had placed a large bet, because it was a *Cert*. The girls didn't know what a *Cert* was.

They had travelled to Ascot in Lochlan's new car, well, not 'brand' new as it was still a few years old, but hey, he reasoned, why pay for depreciation if you can let others. It was a BMW saloon whose leather and walnut interior smelt like the Oxfords Bodleian Library. That's why he bought it. However, he couldn't quite get his head around the fact that the car seemed to have a mind of its own. Letting him know if his seat belt was unlocked or the lights left on, or a door left open. It even bleeped when he reversed the car and he kept thinking he had hit something. He felt completely out of control, feeling as if the car controlled him. He was going to take the car back to the showroom. Mainly because the engine was so quiet compared to his old VW, he didn't know if the engine had stalled and he was pissed off being ordered about by 'the Germans'. The girls thought that it was hilarious and teased him mercilessly by doing a Nazi salute every time he complained at the car.

They had also been 'out on the town', as Rosey called their excursions, to the theatre or comedy clubs, but Rosey did not always go, as the more evident connection Rebecca and Lochlan were nurturing, left her feeling the gooseberry too often. They went to the cinema or bars on several occasions and to a night club, where Lochlan felt so old that he told one sweating gyrating youth that he, Lochlan, was the owner. To be fair, Rebecca felt her age and had also put on a little weight. He had teased her about being plumper, but hey, that's good food for you, he thought, and of course they are seated for several hours a day. Even Lochlan had gained some weight as he was no longer walking to the university via the park and determined to take more exercise.

They made love often. Staring at individual screens for too long made them feel disconnected; to themselves and to the world in general, taking frequent breaks as the work was progressing, mainly because Rebecca was exceptionally efficient and organised. On one occasion she sent his PC an extremely explicit photo of herself, (he presumed Rebecca had taken, but which had been taken by Rosey) with the message *It's all yours Prof* and within a few unzipped seconds his firm manhood stood to attention at her mouth. She tended to prefer giving him that release, at the present time, healthier than yoghurt she used to say, and he wasn't complaining. They did fit well, a bit of sleepy, half-awake penetration in the small hours, his front to her back, both in the foetus position, felt close and loving. She was thinking of three personages in a line and marriage. She even alluded to the possibility during such intimate occasions. He had never thought about marriage or children or living with anyone; ever. He had never considered the idea.

Lochlan had always been confused when his girlfriends used to say, *their* relationship wasn't going anywhere. When he always thought *things* were going along *'quite nicely thank you'*. Marriage, no way. He had made that clear to several women, even when he was following in the wake of R L Stephenson's Island hopping in Polynesia, or the sand prints of Gauguin's amorous footsteps. He had known many clever colleagues get bogged down by family life. The school expenses, the sleepless nights; the trauma and financial consequences of divorce. A promising pool of talent who had never published another thing. No; marriage was not for him in any shape or form. Although he had never had better sex and natural companionship, possibly ever. He resolved to do the work, take the money and let the good times roll. What did Connolly say?

'There is no more sombre enemy of good art than the pram in the hall'

***

The Q tablet's facsimiles, showing the reports, sound-bites and sayings of JC were being translated into Spanish and English initially, partly, Lochlan was informed, because of pressure from the Catholic Church and because Spanish is a language spoken more widely than English, although not so widely read. Eventually of course The Project would be translated into over 30 languages.

A publisher had not been chosen, to avoid any compromising leak, although proofreading of the introduction, (which centred on the Lord Soan's Museum, the history of the origin and discovery of the tablets and the processes that led to the revelations of their secrets) was well advanced. Included was Professor Lochlan Majewski's (BSc Ox: MA. Phil: PhD Auck: B Theol: Dip Con. FRS) verification of the contents, with an eloquent reference to context of which he was duly proud. Only a few people had seen this proof. The whole project was still under wraps. However, mentally he was building up to the book launch with a fair degree of anticipation, as Lochlan genuinely considered the revelations to be little compromised from the original. He was excited, potentially wealthy and had Rebecca. Often.

Uncle Paul phoned his niece.

"Hi Rebecca, I hear from Sotakos that The Project is progressing well and that your work is invaluable. He wondered if you would be able to stay on for the launch. He is not sure how the professor will manage on his own, as he has a tight schedule and will need logistics."

"I don't have a choice uncle, I'm pregnant?"

"Oh! Dear, oh! dear. Are you sure?"

"As certain as red isn't blue."

"I am disappointed, really. You are supposed to be adult about these things. See Tony, he will sort you out, phone him today."

"No, uncle, not this time."

"Oh! dear."

"Yes. No."

"That's a bummer. Is it his, Lochlan's?"

"Yes."

"How come?"

"I missed my weekly shop, and 'the pill' was on my shopping list. Lochy and I went on a pub crawl remember, after your Biker's Café meeting. It was your suggestion."

"Oh, so it's my fault?"

"Quite so. You know. It's… all… your… fuck…ing… fault," Rebecca replied with as much underlying aggression as she could muster.

"Whoa! there, girl. Jesus! I was only joshing. Only joshing you, easy now, easy. Tell me, I was wondering how you were getting along 24/7 with Lochlan; and so was your flatmate, who seems a little jealous, by all accounts. It's a bit full on, isn't it?"

"It's not easy for me, until recently I have felt awful, but had to carry on, faking my periods and all, yet keeping him happy, you know. It's been bloody difficult, no pun intended."

"That's not a pun."

"Stop being so glib. I'm serious uncle. Although it's hardly *a coup de foudre,* I do like him, and he is kind and caring most of the time. He's been great fun, and takes notice uncle; you know, he understands me, even my change of mood or lipstick or hair. When was the last time you noticed or anybody else for that matter? He seems to know what I'm thinking. Its uncanny. His wit is edgy, don't you think? Although his *boom-boom* jokes are excruciating, you still laugh. He has a certain presence, charisma, you know, and his students seem to adore Lochy as he does have a powerful intelligence don't you think? We have had some humdinger discussions on art, politics, religion, you know, everything; and he listens; really listens. Don't worry uncle, I will still go through with the assignment, and I don't know what joshing is, but I don't like it."

"Yes, of course. I'm sorry. There will be a huge bonus in this for you as you know, a considerable amount. Are you sure that you haven't planned this baby? I mean you seemed keen on him from the start. We really can't allow your hormones to influence the outcome. You know what must happen if he knew The Project was a deception." There was a prolonged silence on the phone. "Rebecca... Rebecca... Rebecca," he emphasised her name in a slow ascending drawl, and eventually Rebecca said.

"Yes uncle."

***

Rebecca was bent over the armrest of the large sofa in the lounge, naked from the waist down, with her legs akimbo, her dressing gown hoicked up and with Lochlan thrusting in panting enthusiasm from the rear. Suddenly the lounge door opened and Mel, their cleaner, walked in, but before either of the conjoined party had noticed or moved, she had smacked Lochlan on the arse, playfully, saying "Don't mind me you two" and disappeared into the kitchen to start cleaning. They just carried on, laughing. He was put off his stroke for a time, but he managed to finish, pulling up his boxer shorts, just in time for Rebecca to make it to the toilet. He went into the kitchen to pick up a beer, and as Mel bent down to get a bottle for him from the lower drawer of the fridge, he pulled down her jogging slacks and knickers in one move and smacked her hard on her bare arse in retaliation. She screamed.

He had met her at the Thai Orchid, he knew her *game* of course, but had always found female company preferable to a pornographic wank. And he did have his offers, (mostly free, as the females at 'the students' parties, often outnumbered the males and waited to see who was unfortunate to be left over) which he often declined, as he just found using condoms a complete turn off. One drunken evening however, after getting some lubricated, ribbed wonder condoms from the machine in the Orchid's toilets, he had taken Mel back to his place. Later, after paying her in the end just to let him fall asleep, he awoke, late in the morning, to find that she had cleaned the whole apartment, leaving him a note that read, 'I no take money from you for doing nothing.' After that she was hired.

***

"She is sweet on you Lochy, she love you," Mel said this while rubbing what she would find later was a complete hand print to treasure.

"Bugger off! You must be joking Mel. She is very well paid, you know. Nothing like good money to keep one happy in one's work. No, I don't think so somehow, she is lovely though."

"Yes, she is well sexy. I too skinny for you."

"She works very hard and is incredibly efficient, I couldn't have done this project without her. No way. She's made it easy, and fun. No sir, I have enjoyed the work Mel, normally such a project is purgatory."

"What is purgatory?"

"A sort of self-imposed suffering."

"Yes, I see you like that normally you write."

Lochlan had left the building for his 'Darwin walk'. He called this his thinking time, once around the whole park, or more times if the weather was set fair or his thought process was working overtime. Something he had always tried to do if he had spent some time writing, but he had done so more frequently recently, since his weight gain. He knew that it was down to beer really, but he would rather run daily marathons to lose weight than give up the brew. Or so he told Rebecca.

***

"How long you pregnant, miss Rebecca?"

"Oh my GOD! Mel, how do you know?"

"I am woman, also do laundry."

64

"Please. Please, don't tell him, please."

"Why you not tell him, he good man?"

"It's way too complicated, Mel. Please don't tell him or anyone, please."

"Seems simple. You love him, him love you, he has job, flat. You married?"

"No. It's more complicated than that: please keep our secret. It could be the death of him."

"You are sad. This should be happy time."

"Do you have children?"

"Yes, I have four. No See."

"FOUR!"

"Don't cry."

"Four, why don't you see them?"

"We here, this country, to pay for their good life and education. Don't cry. It's what we do."

"But you don't see them, why leave?"

"No come, they die, so also my mother, who feeds them. My children's life more important than my life. Many in restaurant do this; not just Orchid. My husband chef, he come first long time. He good English speaking, he teach me. The professor teach me also, only rude words. That's better, you laugh."

They embraced on the sofa-bed, Mel held her close. Rebecca was laughing and crying.

"Thank you, thank you, Mel. Thank you. That has put everything in perspective and the cat amongst the pigeons, big time. I will keep this child come what may, no matter what. I am so glad you came today. That's what I needed, Mel, a little perspective."

"You must Miss Rebecca, you must. Listen. I was asked to give information about the Professor, to someone."

"Oh shit! When? Why?"

"Long time now. Not lately asked for."

"How, why, by whom? Who asked you to spy?"

"No spy, he just want information."

"Who? What? Mel."

"Man used to come to Orchid to know if the professor do drugs and things."

"Dark hair, motorbike, tattooed, leathers."

"Yes."

65

"Did he pay you?"

"No, he just ask and eat and tip big. He ask if he crack-head or fucked kids or was drunk shit head. I told him truth. Professor is good man, kind man, very funny, but no crazy. Biker not good man, has now Dianne."

"Did you tell Lochy about him?"

"Yes, he seemed pleased, he said man want Dianne."

***

The book launch was the most amazing success, billed quite rightly, as the most Exciting Religious Discovery in History, Pre-launch orders had already totalled 500 million. Crowds waited at the major book stores in several countries and tech savvy persons had ordered large numbers online. Offering the books at a discount. Especially religious organisations. There were also some individuals and companies who wished to produce a film of the events leading up to the discovery of The Tablets, but any requests were denied.

This phenomenon was perhaps also a reflection on Professor Lochlan Majewski's observations when invited onto The BBC's Breakfast Show. *To have a beautifully bound book in one's possession, in one's pocket even, that embodied a copy of J C's actual teaching and sayings, the actual words, may be preferable to reading them as an E-book or web page. The printed word on Paper has made a huge contribution to the progress of mankind and will continue to do so. As indeed has ink on parchment and vellum. It was the physically inscribed words that made the discovery of Q possible. It will also be available on-line in over 30 languages eventually.*

Sales of his own academic publications had soared and 'Conversations' about the publication of Q via the social media had gone 'viral' and international. There was even an extensive waiting list for his book on the Historical Processes and Development of Paper Making and Printing in Polynesia, as The University Press could not respond to the demand. Normally the University's Academic Press publications would not sell their print run. His facile answers when questioned by sceptics, (who doubted the authenticity of the actual eye witness accounts of The Miracles e.g.) were often quoted. When asked, for example,

"Do you not think Professor, it's inconceivable Jesus was the very first person to stand on higher ground that looked out over the Sea of Galilee and seen the silver flicker of shoals of fish just under the water?"

He replied, "Not really, it's a feasible explanation, but when people are only just self-sufficient, they are busy getting on with trying to survive. Subsistence fishermen may well just get up every day and do what they do, as their ancestors did, mend nets, tar their boat and fish on the water; blindly doing what their father and grandfathers did before them. The idea of a lookout, way up on the cliff or higher ground telling them where to fish, pointing out the flickering sunlight on the silver of the shoals, may never have occurred to them. Of course, when some clever bugger like Jesus thought of it, they took it to be a miracle. Even Ireland for example, hadn't discovered the lobster pot as a method of entrapping encrustation until the end of the 16th century, although most Mediterranean country's had centuries before. Irish fishermen just kept on doing what their forefathers had done, until some Spaniards washed up on the Irish coast from the Armada and spilled the beans."

***

"Hi, uncle Paul, I'm worried. I need to see you as I'm fairly certain that I am being followed, and I want to see you now."

"What's the magic word Becky?"

"Uncle: please. I'm no longer 15."

"Okay. Sorry Beck. When, where, why?"

"I want a day out, like we used to have."

"Do you have anywhere in mind?"

"Yes. WC2A 3BP."

"Rodger, got that. Thursday at one would suit?"

"Yes, okay, me too. Thursday at one is good for me."

"Are you sure you're being followed as you were way paranoid in Paris, remember? You found every shadow menacing."

"I know, I know, but I'm certain?"

"Absolutely."

"Definitely?"

"Okay. Will do. Fresh garb then."

"Yep, all though tad excessive uncle, best to; don't you think?"

"All right, Becky and don't worry. It's not the same situation as Paris, I know, but it's best to be cautious. See you lunch time tomorrow."

***

"Sorry I'm late, had to find a new suit. All the rest were all a bit small waist wise. What's this all about my dear?"

"No worries, we can't enter now as we have to queue anyway. They only allow a few people in at any one time, which is a good idea, don't you think?"

"Yes, I hate crowded museums, you cannot see any object clearly through the people and I resent the fact that so many people have had the same idea as me."

"It must make you feel *so* ordinary, uncle? You're such a snob."

"As you look so lovely, I will forgive you your jibe: have you checked everything you are wearing?"

"Yes, everything, which were bought this morning. Mel uses the washing machine at the Orchid for our clothes and you said trust no one."

"It does seem a bit excessive I know, but we cannot be too careful. You're not listening Becky."

"Sorry…memories of the Ninth Arrondissement."

"Don't you fret, my love, it's not the same. Come on, it's our time to go in: leave the umbrella outside in the porch."

They entered the most amazing labyrinth of eclectic artefacts from all over the world, but especially from those countries bordering the Mediterranean. Every nook and cranny of a large gentleman's residence of five floors was bursting at the seams with curios, large and small. Some were valuable, as were some of the paintings by Canaletto, including a huge glass topped Egyptian sarcophagus, containing the mummy. The Sir John Soane's Museum, Lincoln's Inn Fields is an emporium of one man's obsession with possession. Soane was a well to do architect, much given to knocking down the walls and even floors of his residence and even completing the same restructuring on the adjoining house which he purchased when he had run out of space. Although undoubtedly one of the most atmospheric experiences in London, Rebecca was intent on locating Lord Soane's stacks of Roman tablets that allegedly contained Q.

Rebecca was thorough in her research and had discovered that the Q tablets were to be returned to the museum after they had been scanned at The Imperial College of Engineering in 2003. On enquiring from the curator of the Soane's Museum, (who was ensconced on the third floor) she was informed that they were officially requested by The National Archive Office and never returned. Further enquiries ascertained that the N.A.O. had no idea where they were. None of the day to day incised Judea administrations tablet records were extant, apparently. *We now only have the scanner images*, she was told. Her uncle had not followed her upstairs, as there was no lift, and waited anxiously in the foyer.

"There you are uncle, that was convenient."

"What was?"

"They are lost. As if you didn't know, and don't pretend you don't know what's disappeared."

"Well, I'm not surprised, I have been led to believe they looked like solid ridged drain pipes, totally nondescript and uninteresting. They are probably hard core somewhere, caretaker's driveway I shouldn't wonder."

When they left the museum, he opened the umbrella, as the rain was still torrential. Realising the one umbrella was unable to provide shelter, they walked quickly to the park bandstand that was opposite the museum. They had to shout over the drumming of the rain on the tin roof.

"Hey! that's not my umbrella."

"No matter it's much the same. Anyway, it could be bugged. Everything we are wearing is new as a precaution and you bring an old umbrella. It's why I left it outside the museum and didn't pick yours up. We are supposed to be professional Rebecca. You should have learnt by now."

"Stop telling me off. I liked that umbrella, it wouldn't have transmitted anything worthwhile in this noise, and anyway, we are not professionals, not really, are we?"

Uncle Paul Smith (aka Rabbi Cohen) made a palms up gesture of compliance, revealing the treasured gold cuff links that he always wore, he didn't want to aggravate her further as he was intrigued at her Q Tablet quest, although he knew of course that she had rumbled the scam, not very difficult from her perspective, but how much she really knew, he wasn't sure.

The rain eased a little, so they walked arm in arm to the restaurant in the park huddling under the umbrella. The restaurant was almost empty. A surly waitress took their order for a pot of Earl Grey Tea.

"You look ravishing Becky, you really do, you are glowing."

"Well that's pregnancy for you, and you can't sweet talk me any more uncle. I have grown up. You no longer have any influence over me, thankfully. I feel a great liberation as I no longer care if you like what I am wearing or my hair or my opinion. And I no longer care what you think about anything. Ever since I fell in love with *our* professor, my regard for you just vanished overnight, on the first night as a matter of fact, what orgasms." She stared at him. "Yes plural." She wanted to hurt him.

"So?"

"I have a growing love for my child, I am in love with his father and I want to marry him."

"Now hold on. Where the hell did that come from?"

"I want this baby and I don't need your permission to marry, because you are no longer my guardian as I am now old enough to be beyond your jurisdiction, even in the States, but I really do need your assistance, I want some honesty, and this is my main reason for calling you; for being here." Faltering, she drew breath, brushed one hand through her hair, whilst picking at the tablecloth with the other. "I want to know, we want to know, what your Brethren, your devout Christian Brothers, have in store for us. That's Lochy and me."

Rebecca's uncle was slow to respond as he was not at all sure how to react. After some time, he decided to reverse the question.

"What does he know? More to the point what do you know he knows?"

"Nothing, nothing at all, he truly believes that the Q tablets were genuine and The Project was pursued with great integrity and he has been overwhelmed by 'the media', although, thrilled by the global response. How else would he have convinced the doubters, who were conducting voice and facial tests, especially on the eyes, to detect any flaw in his innocent presentation while interviewed. He thoroughly checked out your Brethren's tale of the Q tablets when he returned from your induction process, and he found the Lord Soane's tablet stacks were authentic and everything tallied with what they said was put out in Academia, as it were, including the dates, and he was not at all suspicious of fraud because your Brethren are so eminent and learned and spiritual."

"I want the truth … The absolute truth."

She leant forward and stared at him with her cold brown eyes. Her resolve and determination bore deep into his heart. "The teachings and sayings of Jesus were never ever part of the incised information in Lord Soane's tile stacks, were they? All the information discovered via the scan did not include anything to do with Jesus or his followers?"

Uncle Paul, reverted to type, (the nervous actor unsure of his lines) and hesitated. He knew what Rebecca's unflinching stare meant, tell me the truth or I will ruin you.

"No. Becky." He leant forward, "They were not." He waited for a second to gauge her reaction, but she did not blink; although she flushed with fear. "Not one, the whole process, including Lochlan's induction was, and still is, a complete and utter fabrication."

She sat back, continuing to hold his gaze coldly.

"How many people know?"

"Seven, eight now, including you. But it's difficult to prove. I don't think anyone would take you seriously. It is so big now and so believed, globally. Even the Pope has endorsed it, for Christ's sake! *Je grober die luge, desto einfacher ist die tauschung.* As Joseph Goebbles famously said."

"I know, '*The bigger the lie the more it will be believed.*' I wasn't thinking of exposing the scam uncle, far from it. I am more worried that the lost tablets will turn up and be scrutinised and I am even more concerned that Lochlan will find out about the huge scam, and how he was party to a great fucking lie that was a futile attempt to stem the tide of Christian indifference. If he finds out that he was duped by you, me and the Brethren; it would destroy him. He would probably top himself. Now that would be convenient, all too convenient. I need to know who knows. I need to know, that everyone involved, are irrevocably locked into the secret. It will be way too difficult to keep this

71

from coming out. You understand uncle. I'm frightened, so frightened and I was so happy."

"Well; we all are all locked in Becky, all of us."

"All of us. I mean whose idea was it anyway?"

"I'm afraid I wasn't given a name, I was only told, the person who proffered the idea to the incumbent Pope, was a most senior British politician. The Brethren said he conceived the idea once the scanner imaging of Lord Soane's tablets had been declared a success at Imperial College and he had been informed or read that day to day records from the time of Christ had been found. It was world news, that was the type of headline that inspired him, apparently. He was on the blower to the then Pope immediately, but the Pope incumbent flatly refused to endorse the planned deception. Later the said prominent politician had an ordinance with the Pope Elect who endorsed the plan unequivocally and it was set in motion, unfortunately several years later, from the very day the white smoke rose from the Vatican chimney."

"And you and your flock would be disgraced and defrocked and excommunicated, would they not, even if they only just thought of bleating?"

"That is so, Becky. We are all locked in, there is no need to worry."

"Oh, but I do uncle, I do. Did you know Matthew died last week in a motorcycle accident?"

"Yes, I heard. Bike crazy he was."

"But he also knew you had recruited Lochlan, and you and your ecclesiastical Mafioso know that I recruited Lochlan. When all is said and done, he knows, at the very least, that he was set up and I know, the grand payment he is expecting sometime soon, will not happen, could not happen, just in case the information was discerned through the banking system and was perceived as a bribe."

"There is too much at stake for all involved Becky."

"Exactly, exactly: he is going to kick up if he is not paid, he really is. In short. Is he destined to have a 'little accident'?"

"Now calm down Becky my dear girl, you seem to be getting into a state. You seem to think Lochlan could be hanging under Blackfriars Bridge any time soon. Crazy motorcyclists do crash you know? And I understand there was no other vehicle involved."

"I'm just scared. So scared. And not just for me. I just hadn't realised how huge this would be and the financial gain must be colossal, not to mention the vast upsurge in Christian interest and the phenomenal increase in congregations worldwide. It is like the 'Second Coming', uncle. There are many who believe it is a precursor, and he, Jesus, or his disciples, had prior knowledge, and expected that his preaching's would be unearthed, as if deliberately placed in a time capsule. You must have seen them on the news, you must have. Vast numbers, in so many countries are queuing to be baptised. Just imagine the repercussions if the Lord Soane's tablets turned up and were re-scrutinised. Just imagine your after life if that happened. It is much more logical to dispense with the tablets and most of those who had the 'knowledge'."

"Maybe. Maybe. I can see your reasoning. Lochlan, and you and Matthew are the only ones who were not involved from the beginning. Brought in as facilitators, so to speak. And we, including myself, are the only persons with knowledge that are outsiders. I see that. We see that. Lochlan could tell his story in all innocence because he thought, and what's more, is convinced as you say, that all our clandestine activity was to protect The Project before publication. Yes, we do see that. I have always comprehended that possibility."

"Always?"

"Yes Becky, always, from the very beginning in fact. Although I hadn't predicted, well no one predicted, such an overwhelming response to the book's publication. I promise you that you have no need to worry."

"I do hope you are right uncle, I so do hope you are."

"Shall we order something, you need to feed my nephew and we almost have the place to ourselves as it's still raining cats and dogs. I think some wine is needed."

"Sorry uncle, I am off alcohol." She tapped her tummy.

"Ah, yes of course."

"And what's with those 'cats and dogs'?"

"I honestly don't know why we say that."

"And sometimes it's raining 'stair rod's'."

"Now that makes more sense, Becky."

The waitress was summoned and they both decided on the plat de jour. Uncle Paul ordered an Oyster Bay white wine, because Lochlan had told Becky that it was one of New Zealand's finest. She decided to risk a glass. The waitress was more convivial having a mind to a potential tip from the diners; seldom procured from the *just tea* drinkers.

"I am glad that you are in love, as you say you are, I am truly pleased for you, and I like him, yet, I'm not sure why. Although he comes across as genuinely unprejudiced and self-effacing for a boffin. But I must say, I wasn't expecting you to fall for him, Beck. Love is love, however, and knows no boundaries... *although, you were from the outset, just meant to befriend him, fix the deal and depart; as you well know... and not to blow bloody doors off.*"

Rebecca laughed. He did a passable Michael Caine impression. She had always enjoyed his company, although some would say that she had good reason to hate him: thoroughly.

"It has caused problems for The Christian Brotherhood I am sure, but I was not included in their detailed planning. I was given my remit and with yours and Mathew's assistance, we have succeeded and I or you have no further part to play as far as the Christian Brotherhood is concerned."

"Exactly, uncle. Exactly."

The food had arrived and after the usual formalities of proffering the condiments and complementing Lochlan on his wine recommendation, uncle Paul resumed the conversation.

"I do see what you mean. I do see."

"You must have given some thought to the eventual outcome of your involvement uncle, you must have. You must realise that they have used you and your connection with me. You have been involved in one of the biggest religious scams, if not the biggest scam in history."

"Possibly; although you would never know, in fact, no one would comprehend how all-encompassing a scam may be if a public deception was totally successful. Q seems to be completely accepted globally. As are some questionable Rembrandt's, as you know."

"That's different. It only changes the value, although the image stays the same. Which is nuts I know. This scam is entirely different. Take the Christian Brethren's fucking motto for starters.

It makes me wonder if we will get past first base. I know that you were blackmailed into being involved and that your acting career and reputation were on the line. I knew that. I understood your difficulties, but you're obviously a convincing Rabbi."

"Thank you, luckily your predecessor, Dianne, reported that he rarely watched films or TV, and I can do religious intonation. Vicars and co are bread and butter to actors, even a career for the lesser talented."

"It's not the national theatre uncle, it's seriously fraudulent. I was naïve. I had no idea. That's why I said yes, eventually. You persuaded me. I felt obligated to assist you in a grand deception, as you put it. Because, you came for me, after ma and pa died. Found me and rescued me from Zak. You sorted me out, I owed you uncle, big time, you knew that. I had no idea how mega this was going to be, no idea; not an inkling. I was only doing you a favour, as you had done so much for me, and I felt needed. Although I did wonder why you had offered to pay all my study fees and flights and the rental for an apartment. It did seem excessive, and so I thought your project was obviously important. I understood that I would be assisting a professor to be party to an illegal scheme, in which you had a character role, but you never said that my life would be on the line."

"I never considered it to be so Becky, believe me, I am far too fond of you, you know that. I still do not believe it is, for anyone of us, but, especially you, a likely outcome. You were co-opted as there was an immediate need for a substitute, I wouldn't have suggested you to the Brethren if I didn't believe that I could fully protect you."

"Are you sure, uncle Paul?"

"Positive." Uncle seemed preoccupied with his thoughts for a few seconds and continued. "It does make sense, you could be right. You have got me thinking about Matthew, I wasn't sure why he was chosen, quite an unsavoury character, don't you think? I will need to send someone to see or phone Dianne and get more information on the exact circumstances of his accident. Apparently, she was at the scene. I can't think of anyone else we can trust with our enquiry, as I was told that she was unaware of the Q element when she moved in with our Professor. It was just another profiling assignment."

"I could do it."

"I didn't know that you knew him that well?"

"I don't, and I don't know Dianne either, but she knows that I am shacked up with her ex. I could call and say that Lochy had heard about Matthew's death and commiserate."

"Does Lochlan suspect that Matthew was instrumental in creating an opening for you when he seduced Dianne?"

"No, not at all. He was pleased that she had left and thought even less of her choice of partner, apparently. He told me … *anyone who wears an air and watertight suit, plus gloves and a visored-helmet, just to travel, while making as much noise as possible, should go to the fucking moon."*

He smiled at Lochlan's comment, but he also noticed his niece was reminiscing and smiling. She might be in love, he realised.

"I told you he's an intelligent, unassuming, genuine, lovely, regular guy. He's a bit bonkers at times, but who isn't? He is the first real nice guy that I have been with for this long, I don't usually do nice, do I? You know that uncle. He's so very considerate and he trusts everyone, including me, and I feel so guilty, so, so, fucking guilty."

"About skipping the pill?"

"No! You, dickhead! About everything. Deceiving him. It *was* an accident," she said emphatically, "I forgot that I hadn't taken the pill, otherwise I would have taken the 'morning after pill'."

"Now relax Becky, it's going to be okay. But you are quite right to be concerned as we are dealing with some extremely powerful and clever people, whose reputations would collapse if the genie was out of the bottle. In fact, the whole ethos of Christianity would be shattered. That is a high price to pay for failure. So maybe we should take their motto seriously. I agree with you, I thought that I could just take the money and walk away. You should phone her. I have Dianne's, but only her mobile number, and I have Matthew's, but only his home number, she may still live at his place."

"Shall I phone now?"

"No, perhaps not. On second thoughts, if you are right about being followed, we had better phone from a kiosk, don't you think? Safer all round, as we don't know with whom we are dealing, now that everything has gone global. '*Per Omnes et Omnis Medium*'."

Uncle left more than enough money to cover the bill on their table, and as the sun had broken through the cloud and promised a warm evening, they decided to walk towards a telephone kiosk on the other side of the Lincoln Green.

***

In accordance with their Will and Testament, uncle Simon Cohen was her parent's guardian of choice after Flight AM69 went down over Greenland with 'all hands'. Middle East terrorism was suspected, but unproven. Rebecca was at a female boarding school in Paris at the time, although she eventually, after an untimely break, continued her studies in England until she had finished her Baccalaureate. Vacations were occasionally spent with her uncle Cohen, her mother's only remaining sibling, especially when he was filming, or on stage in Europe. He had taken on his role as her guardian, reluctantly, feeling inadequately prepared as he had not had children, or often been in their company, except on set or stage. After his recent health-check he had been more circumspect and about his responsibilities as her guardian. He had taken his role seriously once he had a settled relationship with partner, Peter, a lawyer, who had suggested, as Simon was the only adult male family member in Rebecca's life, he was privileged.

All the park benches were damp and steaming in the warming air, and as there was nowhere dry to sit, they walked slowly, to walk and talk, and also, so the pace was easier, as she realised her uncle was struggling with his fitness, not something that was apparent to her in the Soane's Museum. Or maybe I was too preoccupied and anxious to notice, she thought.

"You must hate me sometimes, Becky. I seem to have involved you in something that has mushroomed beyond my wildest imaginings."

"Well, it's not the first time that you have involved me in your wild imaginings."

"I guess I did take advantage of your youth and vulnerability? I'm not sure what came over me or how it happened."

"Yes of course you do, you, old codger. The hashish helped you, I guess. I took advantage of your age and experience, it was me who slipped into your bed, remember? And I needed cuddles. I was desperate and you came and found me, you came for me. I was grateful."

"Yes, of course. I remember; everything. I have never been so scared or felt so protective. I kept thinking I must look after you, as it's what my sister would have expected of me. You needed to get back to ground zero, to come down, to kick it. The 'pot' smoking was part of my plan to ease your journey, I had to join in. I smoked it a lot in my youth, which I had to curtail as I began to forget my lines, strictly frowned upon professionally, of course."

"I was in such a state, wasn't I? It must have been so difficult for you."

"Yes and no, I was *resting* between acting jobs, which gave me a timely break and my last film had paid well."

"The barge trip was part of your grand plan to keep me from seeking out my crack head fiends, I realised that later, much later, for it wasn't an easy situation for either of us, and it was bloody cold on the water."

"Wasn't it just? The canal was frozen solid, remember? the locals were even skating. A fine Barge Holiday that was. How long were we stuck in Paris on the canal Saint-Martin?"

"For nearly two weeks, I think, although it's a bit of a fuzzy memory."

"That's good *grass* for you."

"I loved it, it was so homestead, with that log burner and all, it was a sensual re-awakening, you know, like we girls felt at school. You were kind and considerate. Zak was a brutal lover, as you found out."

"You were in a bad way Becky, although lucid and talkative between bouts of vomiting and crying; that's when you told me about the drug drop, and Zak's pick-up time as well."

"In Dieppe. Did I tell you that?"

"Yes, you kept insisting, screaming in fact, that you had to go with him to Dieppe to meet The Lullaby, because you loved Zak. You were meant to go with Zak, because he loved you. To go on board The Lullaby, because Zak said you had to. That's why I threw your cell phone down a drain. That's why I was able to tell the police where their drop was and the name of the yacht."

"You, old bugger uncle, I never knew, you never told me. No wonder Zak's Gang were after us. After you kidnapped me and I was missing, I assumed his gang always thought it was me."

"They probably did, but kidnap is too strong Becky; I persuaded you to come to the barge."

"Handcuffed with electro binders?"

"Well, you were quite out of it, to tell the truth. They picked Zak up with Marek as you know, but I also never told you, the gendarmes who made the arrests discovered that you were meant to go back to The Caribbean with the yacht's crew as part payment for the drugs, along with Marek's girl. To be used and abused on the voyage and probably thrown overboard at some point, they assumed."

"Oh my God, I could be dead, we could be dead, although I never liked Marek's girl Zoe, she was so fat, they probably needed her for ballast."

"Meow! Meow!"

"Well, she was a big girl. Why have you never told me all this, not even when we were on the run."

"I didn't want to worry you unduly. Zak's mates were after us and you still declared your love for him, looking for any opportunity to abscond. I wasn't sure how you would respond if you knew. *You put him on a pedestal and he put you on the game.* Was a succinct line from your therapy report, which I thought rather summed up the whole affair, don't you think?"

"The therapists had a line in stock phrases, often that's all you got. Such as *'he sold you on',* although I still thought that I loved him. I was always precocious. You always said, even when I was little."

"Did I, gosh. Yes, you certainly were a most vivacious young girl, and quite a performer, singing, dancing, piano. Making up plays, that you forced your friends and family to join in, including me."

"Really? I can't remember too much, did I upstage you?"

"I suspect that you may have. You certainly did on 'our' barge. It was an initiation for me also, as you probably realised at the time. I wasn't familiar with the female body."

"That's so funny, it didn't matter, and it wasn't expected. I don't think that I wanted more than affection, it was all about cuddles and closeness and our games. I guess that even in Paris you knew which side your butter was spread, it was always *The Last Tango* with you. That's so, so, funny."

"Well, I never really noticed girls as I grew, friends used to have posters of female pop stars on their bedroom walls, while I had Cliff Richard and Adam Faith."

"Yes, of course I knew your predilection, but, until I met Lochy, you were all I had. It doesn't make sense I know. When I disappeared from school; several weeks after I flew back from Ma and Pa's funeral. I was not in a good place, an emotional wreck really, I see that now. '*You have lost your anchors*' my therapist said."

They found a seat which had been more sheltered, but still close to the telephone kiosk, and sat down; a palpable exhale of relief emanating from her uncle.

"I know Beck, but nor was I."

"We both were, sadly, and I met Zak at La Palaise day-time disco in the Rue Poissonniere. The ideal hang out for Parisian night workers, recovering, hung over dropouts and prostitutes. And did we and his friends dance: to exhaustion. I know, I know, I was young, but in some ways quite adult. I always had to travel to wherever Ma and Pa were on the globe, often on my own, as you know, and soon after I went AWOL. I met Zak and fell in love, at least I thought that I had. My first love, it was all con-suming, but it was too soon after their deaths. I was '*clutching at straws*' as my therapist put it."

"That's understandable Beck, but the school went berserk. They admonished me when I turned up."

"Not really. I wasn't the first teenage girl to abscond from that school; or to shack up with a Punk. They were worried about their money. The US government's payments stopped immedi-ately, apparently, and when I told them that, you, my now guard-ian, were in Patagonia filming a Welsh speaking Western, and that I honestly didn't know when you would be back in Europe; they didn't believe me; especially, as they tried to contact you, but had no joy."

"I came as soon as I heard, as soon as I knew. We were miles from anywhere with a telecom signal. It's fairly remote and there is probably more hardware on the moon than in parts of Patagonia."

"I know uncle, but my therapist said that I probably felt abandoned for the third time, as I probably had assumed that you had known and when the weeks went by and no one could locate you, I was on my own again. I was desperately alone, desperate. I can still recall the sensation, there was such a weight of loneliness. I had no one, even my closest girlfriends left me alone to grieve as most of the staff chose to."

"It was nearly a decade ago, please don't make me feel worse than I do anyway for involving you in the Q scam. I would have told you all about this, years earlier, but your first therapist advised me to forget, as she hoped you would."

"I don't mean to blame you, you're all I have left. But I would still like to thank the lady who took me in to her room the first night that I was alone in Montmartre. I have only thought of her again, recently, since, you know, my child to be. I was so young, I know that now."

"Yes of course you would. You were lucky she sheltered you, sleeping 'on the street', in your school uniform, no less, would have been fraught with danger; but on the other hand, the police may have picked you up and things could have panned out differently."

"If anything happens to me uncle, promise me you will try to find her; promise. She was a concierge for one of the houses that flank the small garden behind the Follies Bergere. I was sleeping in the garden."

"Yes, I know, but you said, at the time, she was elderly, it was almost a decade ago, she's probably dead, A situation you are not likely to be in anytime soon. Calm, Becky, doucement. You are going to be fine."

"I hope you are right. I really, really do, although the outcome of our involvement is far from certain. You probably took on the Rabbi role as a challenge."

"Not really, my promiscuous history caught up on me. Did you know? The Vatican City's legal age of sexual consent was twelve years of age until just a few years ago? I should have become a real Cardinal rather than a fake Rabbi, then my reputation could not be potentially besmirched as was threatened."

"Oh dear, I am so sorry, I never realised that you never had any choice but to be involved in this awful Q thing. Although I knew something was up."

"Does that bit of information make you regret our barge exploits Beck?"

"No. I don't regret our mutual adventure."

"You had a very boyish figure then, I guess. Anyway, we did have fun."

"Yes, absolutely. The born actor in you was so convincing, and I was mature enough to want to be convinced, if that makes sense? No, I don't hate you, in some ways I am grateful. The animosity that you have picked up on is more to do with getting involved with this Jesus scam. It's so big, it will get us all killed. I am fairly certain that I am being followed as you know and something you said earlier makes me think that our apartment is bugged."

"Yours and Rosey's?"

"No. Silly. Our apartment, Lochy's and mine."

"I see."

"Yes, well, don't look at me like that. It's just that sometimes I just want to run away with dear Lochy and play happy families; but I can't tell him why and anyway we would be found, eventually, wouldn't we? Uncle Paul. Wouldn't we?"

"Now *you're* being very silly."

Part Two

Rebecca was awakened by a loud frantic knocking sound on the side window and as she opened her eyes her whole vision was filled by a face, at close quarters, she could see the features clearly, of a dishevelled white male, sporting a moustache, beard and dreadlocks, in the reflected light from the dashboard.

"Are you okay Miss?" he shouted in a broad Geordie accent. "Only I saw the pipe, shall I phone for an ambulance?"

"No, don't, don't, and who the fuck are you and where the fuck am I?" She was shaking uncontrollably and felt like vomiting.

"Open the window, Miss, you'll need some fresh air, I won't hurt you," his voice faded as he went to the other side of the car, and moved around to the car's passenger door; instinctively Rebecca went to lock the car door, although it was already locked, so she unintentionally unlocked it in her panic.

Banging her hands hard on the steering wheel, she shouted, whilst coughing and gasping for air. "No, for fucks sake. Go away. Fuck off." Never having experienced at any time, a similar situation. It was incomprehensible, as if emerging from a dark asthmatic dream. She considered the possibility that she may be dyeing. Which, in fact, a few minutes before, she was.

Seizing his opportunity, the young man opened the side door, and ran quickly away and out of the tunnel. Opening her side door, she tried to jump out from the car, but found that she had no strength and was restrained by her seat belt. She felt groggy and sick from the still toxic fumes. She thought of the child, her child. She knew that she had to get to a doctor, a hospital or a clinic. "Tony," she said out loud. "I must get to him."

With no longer a thought for her situation, or seeking any rational explanation for her predicament, she responded to her overwhelming urge to know if the child she was carrying was safe. She turned the ignition key. Lochlan's old car started, but just as she tried to reverse out of the archways tunnel, clattering the gears, the engine stuttered, spluttered and cut. Each time she tried, she had the same result. After deciding to abandon the car, and with the windscreen wipe cloth held over her nose and mouth, she searched for some money in her jacket pockets, the car's side pockets, glove compartment and even under the seats. No notes or loose change for a bus or taxi could be found. Suddenly she noticed that the clothes that she was wearing were not hers. Some person or persons must have undressed me, and put these on, she realised. "Uh! Oh my god!" she exclaimed.

Desperate, Rebecca left the car and ran towards some distant lights as she had no idea where she was or how she had ended up in a dark tunnel, in Lochy's VW, at dusk. She didn't search for answers as she was still in shock. She just kept running towards the light. The road was the service road beside several more railway arches. They had previously housed small businesses, sprouting a non-functioning light over each doorway. The archways seemed to be damp, unused and derelict, and there were sounds within. Scurrying sounds: rats or cats or something, and echoing footsteps, possibly her own or maybe not. A freight train clanked rhythmically above her on the rail track, it seemed to mimic her strides. She had no idea where she was heading, she just wanted to get into the light.

As Rebecca ran closer to a main road, she could see that the last archway contained a Maxi-Taxi operation, which she entered breathing heavily and startled when she saw, half a dozen swarthy Asian men sitting on old car seats in the bright, cold neon lit interior. She found the men disconcerting as none would make eye contact. She addressed the man behind the desk.

"If I give you this gold ring will you take me to Dr Anthony Martin's clinic, Harley Street, please. I have no money with me." No one uttered a word, but now they all looked at her. "It's a sapphire… diamond… gold… it was my mother's… they found it in the wreckage… it's the only thing they found," she was breathing and speaking in gasps. He did not answer, no one answered, they just stared. "For security, I would want it back, when I pay you. I am pregnant. I need to see a doctor…I need to know… if my baby is all right."

The desk man asked if she had phoned the police and after he had understood that she had nothing, but the clothes she was wearing and a ring, he offered to phone for her. She said no emphatically and with such finality that it was not pursued further.

"You must come with me," the deskman said as he gestured to one of the men to take over the office. "My father is a medical doctor. You are obviously stressed, and we will see if everything is all right."

He gave her the most reassuring smile, and this alone enabled her to acquiesce and follow him out of the office and down the main road. He didn't say a word as he had assumed that she was a prostitute recently involved in a client fracas. She was just beginning to question what the hell she was doing walking off with a stranger, when he indicated that they had arrived. It was a private clinic and after the son had said a few words in Punjabi to the receptionist, she was shown inside. The clinic was extremely well appointed and much larger than the frontage and the reception area had implied.

A scan showed all was well with the baby. She could see his little heart beating, but her blood pressure test showed it was too high. The doctor had also ascertained that she may have been drugged, and to have inhaled carbon monoxide, so he decided to keep Rebecca in the clinic overnight, offering a private room, with a phone and television, She was exhausted and overwrought and yet so relieved, she didn't need persuading. A young nurse came in and took several blood tests to be analysed, before giving her a sedative.

Rebecca needed to collect her thoughts and try and work through her amnesia. She was still confused, troubled and in shock. The last thing she remembered was being squashed into a telephone kiosk with her uncle on the corner of Lincoln Fields Green. She was trying to figure out why she was found in Lochlan's 'Marco' as he named his old car, a VW Polo. (He had even had the name professionally 'painted' by transfer, on the rear and on the dashboard by a sign writer.) And why was it parked underneath the railway arches in The Hamlets, a rough area of London? not exactly the Bronx, but racially distinct. And why was she in the driver's seat as she never drove in England? She just couldn't master a 'left hooker' (as Lochlan always referred to driving in the UK). She smiled as she thought of his corny humour, but he did make her laugh, some of his puns were so excruciating, she just had to. She decided to phone him again.

She phoned twice from the clinic with some difficulty as she was still a little shaky. As there was no answer, thinking she had miss-dialled, but after several attempts, she decided Lochy's phone was not receiving calls. Rebecca resolved to try again tomorrow as this was often the case when he was writing, or on his 'thought walk'. She was reluctant to phone her uncle or the police until she had spoken with Lochy first.

She bolstered her pillows and turned on the TV. There was no sound with the picture in deference to the other patients, but there was text. She was watching the news indifferently, as she was still understandably confused, wondering how she had lost three or four hours and then ended up in a tunnel. Sitting up in the bed and adjusting the pyjamas that a nurse had given her to change into whilst explaining pyjamas was a Hindi word. Rebecca was startled into the present. On the TV was her uncle's face, younger, and full screen. She could not comprehend the text. It read:

The death of the character actor Paul Smith was announced today. He is presumed to have had a heart seizure whilst jogging in Richmond Park. There will be a post mortem, but a police spokesman suggested there were no suspicious circumstances.

Rebecca sat more upright in the bed. She was trembling uncontrollably again. She felt the sharp pain of a bursting blood vessel in her left eye. Now she was scared. The acrid smell in the telephone kiosk, came back to her, instantly. She was too stunned to be upset. Uncle never jogged in his whole life, she thought, he didn't even walk fast. He seemed dedicated to indolence. Sure, if he had been running, the exercise would have probably killed him. That her uncle had just died, had obviously registered, but that he was dead, and she would never see him again had not.

Clever lovely uncle, she thought, but jogging; no way; not uncle Paul. Bugger! I will be expected to attend the funeral she realised, and I so want to, she thought, but am I supposed to be dead? A pregnant suicide? And why didn't it work? Or were they just out to scare me *By All and Every Means?* Well they have certainly succeeded. Big time. She felt completely drained by the past 24 hours and very soon her body gave in to her trauma and the sedatives, she curled up on her side with her thumb in her mouth, and fell into a deep sleep.

During the early morning Rebecca began to drift in and out of sleep. What to do? She pondered. Lochlan will see the news or read of uncle's death, but at least his photo looks nothing like his impersonation of Cohen. Maybe I was in the way at the telephone kiosk and they drugged us, killed him, and dumped me. Dumped me in the car out of the way. Maybe it's just coincidence, maybe not. I will try to phone Lochy again she decided. Then she hesitated with the receiver in her hand, wondering why she was found in his car? His Marco. Rebecca only had his apartment number from directory enquiries, her 'whole life' was in her phone.

In the morning she was visited again by the doctor, who informed her that she was suffering from acute hypertension and insisted she remained in the clinic for a few more days. As he had indicated that her baby could be affected, she readily agreed. Where else can I go, she considered, as I have no money and I am meant to be dead. She was understandably depressed and anxious and cried and slept and cried and slept while feeling truly sorry for herself and the loss of her anchor, uncle Paul Smith. Her sadness was also exacerbated by a fear of her and her baby's impending elimination, while also belatedly releasing the heartfelt grief that had been restrained for more than a decade by her emerging pubescence and the need to appear adult and strong after her parent's tragic death.

As a boarder at private schools from the age of five and with her parents frequently residing on another continent. She was unable to grieve for her parent's sudden death immediately. After all, in her eyes she felt abandoned by her parents (her dad especially) from her very first day at school. Later, much later, (after her parent's untimely death) when reading the letters her mother had written to her own mother, Rebecca's grandmother, she understood why her mother had resolved to have no more children; as the first semester of separation from her child, had nearly destroyed her. Rebecca's Mother, never, ever, wanted to let her darling daughter go. She was pleased to be carrying a boy as she had lost both the adult men in her life. There was of course Lochy, but, at this time, she naturally assumed that he was alive and anyway, in some ways, he was more of a child to her.

The doctor was monitoring Rebecca's condition daily as he felt responsible for her well-being and had been alarmed by her constant trauma that manifested in her persistently raised blood pressure. After being confined for almost a week in the clinic, she was awakened very early by the Senior Administrator. He introduced himself and drew up a chair to sit at her bedside. Here we go, she thought hazily, through the dull ache in her skull. Here comes the bill for services rendered. There goes my mums ring.

"The Police are waiting in reception Mrs Majewska. We have no authority to object I'm afraid, as they, the Police, had put out their customary APB, seeking a Mrs Rebecca Vera Majewska, to all the medical establishments within a few mile's radius of your accident; before the rest of the city of London, in general. We are obliged to give names. Is it okay to show them in. Is there anything you would like before I do? We have a clinic lawyer."

"No, no, par problem, but I'm a Mademoiselle, sorry; Miss."

The two short Police officers appeared unimpressive to Rebecca. They were of different gender, but the same size. Bristling with the various accoutrements of uniformed life, pockets, belts, truncheons, radio receivers, personal identity badges; they seemed stocky to her, but then, she was a slender one meter eighty herself. They also referred to her as Mrs Majewska and dismissed her singleton protestations. They asked her to accompany them to Bethnal Green police station where they had apprehended a suspect who may have been near her car. The car found under railway arches near The Hamlets, with a vacuum cleaner hose connected through to the inside, as one would do if attempting a suicide. Of course, Rebecca agreed reluctantly, as she had no choice, and dressed. Noticing that whomsoever had previously dressed her, knew her bra size, Rebecca shuddered at the thought. She was much troubled by her attempted murder, although suicide would have been the obvious verdict. She realised without a shadow of a doubt that she should be dead. She asked the receptionist to thank the doctor and nurses for all their help, and left the clinic escorted by the police. As they left the building her desire for preservation, an animal instinct to survive, for herself and her baby, welled up inside her. I gave my name as Stein to the clinic she realised as they were leaving. *By all and every means.* She thought.

"How do I know that you are police officers? How do I know you are not imposters?" Her voice full of anxiety. "How do I know?"

"Come off it my girl," the female officer said as she opened the rear door of the car. "Where do you think we obtained this full on Police Car, and parked it on double yellow lines without a mind or care for the law? Get in."

***

At Bethnal Green Police station her personal information was recorded by the evening's duty officer and after declaring that she possessed nothing about her person but her mother's ring, she was 'felt up', by a female officer, to make sure. After this induction, which after all was normal procedure, (including the taking of fingerprints and a swab of DNA). Rebecca felt criminalised, demoralised and thoroughly depressed. Everyone who had dealt with her, from the car incident to the present, could see she was traumatised, on the edge and a likely suicide candidate.

After waiting expectantly, she was eventually shown into a bland modern room, (where the chairs and table were fixed to the floor) and sat down opposite two senior detectives and a welfare officer, who gave their names and a welcome. She was shown several images of white men with dreadlocks and picked out Bertram Roberts, showing three views of the unmistakable face of the man who accosted her.

"That's him, that's the man!" she exclaimed.

"Bert, we thought as much. He steals small items and then gives himself up, so that he can spend a night in the warm cells of the detention centre. At Her Majesty's convenience, I may add. He's an 'alky', just after cash. We can appreciate you're upset, Mrs Majewska, do you want to press charges?"

"No, no, it's okay." Rebecca had decided not to raise her profile by questioning their insistence on using her wrong name or pressing charges. She was also resisting the acute desire to tell the officers about everything. About Q, and Lochlan, the Brethren's scam, and uncle and her fears. "I don't think I will, he was not violent, he just scared me. Can I leave please, as I have calls to make."

"We can't do that immediately, Mrs Majewska as we have a few more questions. A few more items you may be able to help us with; anomalies really."

"What anomalies? And I am Miss Stein, Miss Rebecca Stein. I am not married."

"Well that's one anomaly which concerns us. We have clear immutable evidence that you, Rebecca Vera Stein, an American from Melrose Park Chicago, were married to a Lochlan Majewski at Mile End Register Office, last month on the 17th. Hence your marital name and our confusion with the matriarchal addition of the 'A' ending to your surname, in place of the 'I' as all Poles do, we have been informed, for some reason that's 'beyond our ken', this confused us for a while. It took a few days to find you, private clinics being what they are, private that is."

"Well, then. There must be a mix up, I was not there. I don't even know Mile End, and Lochlan was not there either, I'm sure, in fact; certain."

"There were witnesses to your marriage of course, but we haven't contacted them, although we are on the case as it were, so don't worry, it's not illegal to be married. But there is a further anomaly, that concerned us, and we were obliged to investigate your background. As you are the registered owner of the car, we would normally anyway to some extent."

"But, I'm not the owner."

"Well, it is registered in your name at DVLA."

"Los Angeles?" Rebecca was still befuddled.

"No, that's not the LA. It's Swansea. (the officers glanced at each other, both thinking, we've got a right one here.) However, the recent death of Matthew Reynolds, whose number was in the phone found after the unexplained death of your uncle, the actor Paul Smith, has meant our research has been more thorough."

The second officer intervened. He had been staring at Rebecca as if he could eat her and this prompted her to zip up her jacket top a notch to reveal less cleavage. Normally she may have instinctively leant forward, as she had when she first confronted Lochlan in the Orchid restaurant, but, as she felt as tired, unkempt and as undesirable as a rat up a drain, she had no confidence to exude the charm that may have assisted her cause. She was wondering why the original news item suggested that there were *no suspicious circumstances,* but then everything seemed wrong.

"Firstly, we believe you attempted suicide by the inhalation of carbon monoxide via the exhaust of your vehicle, facilitated by a vacuum cleaner hose pipe between the exhaust outlet and the car interior. Is that not so?"

"No. I have no wish to kill myself, or my baby." There were six raised eyebrows. "Yes, I am pregnant." She paused, to steady her fragile emotions and continued after several deep breaths. "This is all so mad, it's madness. I have never, ever, driven that car. Who would have done such a thing?" she asked this question to the officers and to herself. "When he bashed on the window and awoke me, I did not know where I was or how the hell I got there, let alone with a tube up my arse. The last thing I remember is standing inside a telephone box with my uncle, trying to make a phone call. Why didn't it work? Did the young man Bert help someone, or did he do it? Was he involved? I remember what he said, 'I saw the pipe, Miss'."

The detective answered, by suggesting, although Roberts was involved, he had been ruled out as a suspect. The detective went on to say, that no fingerprints were found anywhere in or on the car, except Rebecca's and Bertram Roberts' and Roberts' were consistent with his testimony; therefore the car must have been previously valeted most thoroughly. Which is contradictory to a suicidal state of mind. Also, whosoever fixed up the vacuum tube into the car was a professional, as the tail-gate had been altered to facilitate the plastic pipe from the exhaust into the car. Someone had saved her life, as the tube into the car had been cut, by a person or persons unknown. It could have been Roberts, but he's in denial, and we think it's unlikely.

The second detective stressed, that this fact had led them to believe her innocence in some aspects of the case, and therefore there would be no charge, including trespass, but they were also interested in her relationship to Dianne Mayhew-Robinson who was Matthew's partner and fellow member of The Hackney Harriers Motorcycle Club, whose number was also in her uncle's phone. Rebecca explained that she had no idea why Matthew's number was in his phone as her uncle had hundreds of phone contacts, as professional actors may, and also that she constantly contacted her uncle as he had been her guardian, and why she had given her Marylebone address to the clinic and to the police duty officer when she obviously lived with Lochlan in Hackney,

They seemed to be well satisfied with her answers and she was beginning to relax a little, when they turned off their recording apparatus and informed her that Matthew Reynolds (not his real name) was shot through the heart when travelling down the M40 motorway on his way to the Bulldog Bash near Stratford on Avon in 'The Harriers' thirty plus bike convoy. Ballistics have confirmed that the shot came from a parked vehicle or hiding place as the high velocity rifle would need to be on a tripod or anchored firmly in some way. The coroner's verdict was accidental death, however. On receiving this information, she became sullen and silent.

"Bert has told us that the rear lettering on your car spells Marco. You are not the first person to name a Polo, Marco, as you are probably aware Mrs Majewska, but we have a witness who saw a black VW Polo parked on a parallel road near the scene of the shooting with the same name."

At this point she was caught short as sheer terror coursed through her veins and she only just made it to the toilet, accompanied by a female officer. When she returned to the interview room, the welfare officer, noticed how pale Rebecca looked and asked if she was okay, but as Rebecca had been sick, and found walking difficult, she was shown to a cell. With the combination of all that had occurred in the last few hours she fell asleep almost immediately, but not before she had thought longingly of Lochlan and how worried he must be about her apparent disappearance. She resolved to phone him again.

She was surprised, to be awakened, by the same welfare officer who had put her to bed and now offered her a cup of tea, as she was just finishing her shift and was concerned for her welfare. Rebecca had only slept for a while, yet her thoughts were more focused, noting something amiss in the welfare officer's manner. I guess welfare officers do say that 'they are concerned for your welfare', she thought, but being quite paranoid by this time, she was convinced the welfare officer, was more than she claimed to be. She had told Rebecca, earlier, as she put her arm around her, to steady her, when she walked her to the cell. *Be very careful, remain vigilant and take your opportunity.* Rebecca couldn't fathom the meaning and just nodded in reply, assuming her comments referred to her trauma. She now gave the line more import, and declined the tea, thinking it may be drugged. She realised the Brethren would be able to discern her whereabouts and the welfare officer was not a member of the police force. She had studied the area maps in the police waiting room and noticed the police station was walking distance from Hackney. Sneaking out of the Police Station after she was able to visit the toilets unaccompanied and noting the destinations displayed on the front of buses, (while sensing the general direction) she crossed Victoria Park to Hackney. Rebecca had the strange feeling, she had been allowed to go.

***

Tired and troubled, she arrived at Lochlan's apartment, but there was nobody in. She rang several times, kicked the main door hard in her frustration and cried out his name, but nobody came to the door. The commotion had alerted the always vigilant Mrs Wilson who buzzed the main door open and appeared on the communal staircase that led to her apartment above. She took a disapproving stance, legs planted firmly apart, arms folded across her ample chest, and declared that the occupants of no 12 had 'gorn'.

"Gone, but they can't have."

"Well they have, so there is no point in knocking, changed the lock as well, so I guess that it's up for rent, shouldn't wonder. But I won't have any students in there, I've told 'em."

"I am not a student, Mrs Wilson, I am Professor Lochlan's... ere, wife, you may have seen me before, I live here."

"Now, now, there can't be two of you, my lass. You best be on your way." Mrs Wilson went into her apartment and closed the door.

Rebecca was overcome with confusion, for a moment she even entertained the thought that she may be in the wrong building, although she clearly knew she wasn't. Outside she could see, among the numerous 'To Rent' board signs; number 12 Park View, Lochlan's apartment. Rebecca hadn't noticed when she arrived, as there were always several Estate Agents' boards near the entrance and she certainly wasn't expecting it. Suddenly;

amongst a plethora of emotions, including consummate anger, she was hungry. So, she decided to go to the Thai Orchid, have an early lunch and see if Mel was there and if she knew anything about the apartment. Surely, she thought, Mel would know what was going on with Lochy.

Rebecca thought as she walked. Maybe, she considered, The Brethren had to shut down the apartment, removing any evidence of the scam. Yes, that's it. Maybe, The Brethren have removed Lochy, like they may have removed uncle. Maybe, uncle's death has prompted an enquiry. The police said it was unexplained, she remembered, although the news report said there was no suspicious circumstances. And why his car? Lochy's car, and why registered, to me? Or registered to her, the counterfeit Mrs Majewska.

Lost in her thought, she passed the window of a mirrored barber's shop and caught a reflection of a woman with dishevelled hair, sunken eyes and creased clothing. After a few strides, while her thoughts digested the image, she was slow to realise. Oh! My God! Fuck! It's me... what a mess I'm in, look at me, she thought, mad hair and clothes. Sans make up. She ran her fingers through her matted hair. It needs a hard brush. Bugger! I can't go into the Michelin starred Orchid looking like this, no wonder Mrs Wilson didn't recognise me. Rebecca continued to walk; confused and disoriented, she slipped into the nearest Café, a 'greasy spoon'. She wanted an excuse to use the 'girl's room' and fix her hair. After ordering a black coffee and a 'Big Breakfast', she sat down at an unoccupied corner table having taken the coffee to await her food. Staring fixedly at the chequered table-cloth; thinking about kings and queens, bishops and knights and popes and brethren and how we are all pawns in their games. Only coming out of her trance, when the food arrived. She ate her food quickly. Too quickly. The little bugger must be hungry, she thought. The coffee she drank slowly, trying to think things through. It was quite the worst coffee, but then everything seemed wrong. I need a shower and a change of clothes. I will go to see Rosey at our flat, have a bath and freshen up. I can borrow some money from her. I will take a taxi home to Rosey. But what now? Shit! oh shit, I forgot, I've no money. Shit! She thought, I will just have to try to explain. I will just say that I'll pay tomorrow. Promise to return or something.

She took the bill up to a tall man at the pay desk by the door, handed it to him and while trying to form an explanation, and unable to meet his eye's, she glanced around the Café, and realised, that this was The Biker's Café. Lochlan's Biker Café: then suddenly, on impulse, she ran out of the door and down the High Street; she ran and ran and ran, dodging people with skilful, yet intuitive footwork. She did not look back, not once, she continued to run and run, until she eventually had to slow and pull up, panting furiously, gasping for air; eventually bending over with her hands on her knees, staring at the pavement, wanting to die.

Suddenly he was upon her. He just stood in front of her saying nothing. She was rooted, emotionally drained. He knew she was going nowhere. Then she threw up her breakfast, all over his trainers. He hit her across the head, brutally, with the back of his hand, the blow sent her flying. He was big, and he was strong. He gathered her up. Rebecca felt like a child in his arms. She was hurt, but, wasn't hurting, as the shock had nulled her pain. The sound of pedestrians jeering propelled him along the road at speed. Lunch hour crowds parted as though facing an 'ice breaker', he shot down the alley that was adjacent to his Café, and lifting her over his shoulder, he turned the key, kicked the door open and carried her into a back room. An annexe to the Café. A bedsit. His place. All the way there, the big man kept saying.

"Sorry, I'm so sorry." As tears of remorse and regret welled in his eyes, he placed her in an armchair.

"That's okay. I didn't pay," she said quietly.

"I know, but don't shop me please. I'm a paroled prisoner, a trusty, just working my time, they will lock me up forever, if they find out it was me."

"It's okay. Don't worry."

"Shaun, my name's Shaun," he beckoned her name with a slight rise of his eyebrow.

"Rebecca."

"Are you hurt badly. Rebecca? Do you want some water? Are you a junkie?"

"No," she said indignantly. "Not at all, I've been having a bad time, that's all, I'm a bit disorientated, and broke." Then she told her storey of the past 48 hours, but only the bits relating to her austerity and lack of money or credit cards. He listened with concern, bathing her eye and at one point, kissing her tenderly on the cheek. She didn't flinch as she relished the warmth of his attention and felt once again, childlike. He gave her a few Paracetamol and tried to tell her a joke to cheer her up as he passed her the pills and a glass of water. Having stupidly put his future in jeopardy, he tried to be her friend.

"Why can't you find pain relief tablets in the jungle?" Shaun asked. She just shook her head. "Because ... *the parrots eat them all.*" She tried to laugh, and say *boom-boom*, but a sharp pain occurred in the side of her ear, and she could not. Curled up in the armchair, sucking her thumb for comfort, a lifelong habit when she was feeling sorry for herself, she soon dozed. Shaun returned to his work in his Café through an adjoining door.

When Shaun had finished his stint in his Café, he insisted on driving Rebecca to her flat-share in Marylebone. On the way she learnt that Shaun was a long-term member of the 'Hackney Harriers' and he was in the Bulldog Bash run via the M40 motorway. The consensus from the biking fraternity was that Matthew's death, had been accidental, just a lack of concentration, as there was no obvious reason for his crash. No tyre blowout, or pot hole or prior incident. She asked if there had been a black car parked on or near the hard shoulder of the motorway in the region of the accident. Yes, he said, but it had driven away shortly after the accident. It was on a road that ran parallel to the motorway. He knew for sure, because he had stopped Thor, his motorbike, nearby. Several cars stopped on the hard shoulder after the accident. Some guy had probably just stopped for a pee, or was just curious, he ventured.

"Why do you ask? Were you looking for him in the Café?"

"I knew his girlfriend," she lied.

"Did you. Dianne, One of the Barbies?"

"Yes."

"She hasn't been in for a long while."

Parking outside Rebecca and Rosey's flat share, Shaun was still imploring her not to shop him. Little did he know, she thought, there is no way I'm going near the police again. He thrust some bank notes into her jacket pocket, just as she was sliding out of the car. After leaning across to close her door he drove off tooting his car horn rhythmically.

Rebecca trudged up the outside steps whilst counting the money Shaun had thrust into her pocket. Blood money, she thought as she recalled the incident and the pain, but the moment she stood outside her flat-share her thoughts soon returned to the promise of a hot deep soak in the bath, and bathing her eye and face and washing her hair and telling Rosey, everything. Lochy's apartment only had a shower, a large wet-room with ample room for two as they discovered. She smiled to herself as she recalled, while ringing the doorbell of Rosey's apartment. There was no answer. She banged the door knocker loud while eagerly pressing the bell. Still no answer.

Initially, she was patient, and decided to wait until Rosey returned, sitting on one of the steps, nursing her befuddled head as the intense, but dull ache, returned to her face. She was considering her options, which equated at that moment, to no bath, no hair-wash, no bed, no money and no change of clothes. Then she recalled, with some relief, that she might be away, visiting her parents. That's it, she realised. She may have assumed I was at Lochy's place since we were last in contact. Rosey used to stick a spare key to the underside of the front door mat with a square of Duct Tape when she knew she would be away for some time, so her neighbours could gain access to Rosey's flat and water the plants on the balcony. The arrangement was reciprocal, although her neighbours rarely went away.

As she opened the door, she called out, Rosey, but the sound echoed through every room, empty rooms. Rooms devoid of Rosey's furniture or her belongings. What the fuck has been going on? A stultified Rebecca asked herself. Why has Rosey moved out? Why would she leave without telling me? Although she must have tried my phone and Uncle's of course. She went from room to room opening cupboards, drawers, they were all empty. Who has taken everything? Including Rosey's pictures. Why would she take my things? Maybe the lease ended. But why take every fucking thing including her 'oriental' carpets. Everything. She opened the fridge, in the hope of making an ice pack for the side of her head, the interior was spotless, empty and it wasn't even cold. She tried the lights, nothing. No power. She thought, I've had enough. I just can't take any more, I just can't, but I must be strong, she told herself, I don't want to lose my baby. I must be strong, but I just don't know what the hell's going on.

Over the past few months most of Rebecca's clothes, but by no means all, had migrated to Lochy's apartment, and she was rather hoping for a change of clothes and to borrow money from Rosey, as by this time she was just thinking of buggering off, anywhere, anyhow. Feeling thoroughly deflated, her heavy despondency left her a little as she turned on the hot tap in the kitchen and warm water gushed. She squealed with delight. Of course, she realised, it's a communal system, with the laundry white goods and central heating in the basement, that's why this place is still warm.

The kitchen, the two bedrooms, and a huge lounge led off a long corridor floored now with only bare boards; as were all the rooms. She slipped out of her clothes as she walked towards the bathroom at the far end. I will have a bath, this is still my place, she thought, and I assume uncle, or his Brethren are still paying my half. Of course, he's not now, she realised, suddenly comprehending that she would never see her uncle again; ever. She could feel her tears welling so she focused her thoughts on a potential soak in the bath. Full of anticipation she pushed open the bathroom door. Rosey was in the bathroom, naked: and in the bathwater: naked, eyes open and staring up at her, naked ... and dead.

Rebecca's full-throated screech resounded around the apartment rooms, testing the acoustics of the high ceilings. The shock left her immobile. Rosey's drowned head was pressed hard against the tap end of the bath and her legs were splayed over either side of the free standing, rolled top bath. Her feet were the colour of aubergines, swollen and not dissimilar. There were empty pill packets on the floor and a half full glass tumbler stuffed between her large breasts. The spurting blood from her cut wrists had peppered both sides of the bath and floor and coloured her water. Rebecca just stood there quietly, getting colder all the while, but not thinking clearly, stupidly, she even considered moving her body, so disappointed was she to not be the one in the bath.

Drained of energy, eventually, she sat on the toilet seat, stunned, confused, cold and sickened with fear. She sucked her thumb while rocking slowly, chanting her last school motto *'Age*

Quod Agis, ' (Which she knew meant literally. We must be strong and steadfast.) repeatedly. Her whole head hurt. It was while she was chanting methodically, that she became aware that her chant had synchronised with the drip, drip, of the filling toilet cistern, because the dripping had stopped. Someone must have used this toilet recently she thought. Then realising it had recently been used, jolted her. She knew from experience that the old toilet cistern took several minutes to refill completely and for the final rhythmic dripping to stop. My God! She thought, her killer could still be here, unless it was Rosey who flushed it, in which case she could still be warm. Uh! She knew that she had to get out of the flat immediately and slammed the bathroom door. Suicide? Not Rose, no, not Rosey, she said to herself, not my Rose. Rebecca put her clothes back on in a hurry, although, just before rushing out of the apartment, hesitated, as she noticed the telephone in the hall, and decided to phone Lochy again. She tried, but the line was as dead as Rose.

Rebecca had answered an advertisement for a flat her uncle had seen, and she had phoned and spoken to a Rosemary Gibbs who was seeking a female with whom to share. They met up for an evening drink in the Barley Mow Pub and later, much later, walked to her place. She discovered Rosemary's warm, enthusiastic personality, and similar humour, which pleased her immensely. Although she thought Rosey talked too much. They didn't leave until 'closing time' as they had got on so well immediately. There was an extra bedroom for Rebecca, but after the second night, she shared Rosey's bed, as Rebecca was unable to sleep alone, needing company and cuddles, – *compensating for her loss of family* – her therapist said. Rosey was always there for her, she realised, thoughtfully. Always pleased to see her and often cooked some lovely meals. And they talked about everything. No subject was off limits, (Apart from Q. Which was never discussed) including her pregnancy, (of which Rosey was aware before Mel) and possible termination. She wanted Rebecca to live with her permanently and bring the child up together, but this was something she never considered as she most definitely wanted to marry and live with Lochlan. At least, this is what she told Rosey.

Rosey was more like a loyal pet that needed petting, more comforting, than a long-term relationship. She was fond of her and had hoped to know her forever. 'I'm sure going to miss her', she realised. Rosey had objected to her intended move to Lochlan's place, explaining tearfully, as if there was a bereavement, how she felt strongly that she was her true soulmate, and she loved her – which was very disconcerting – even offering to pay for a taxi to and from her work with Professor Lochlan, as she was so keen for her to continue to stay overnight with her. Uncle Paul had endorsed the commuting idea, but Rebecca was too taken with Lochy to oblige. She resolved to find Lochlan, confront him with all her love and his baby and somehow get as far away from all this madness as possible.

Disappointed, disorientated and troubled. *What to do, what to do, what to do?* She chanted, suddenly bursting into uncontrolled laughter as she heard her cockerel cry and kept crowing and laughing for several minutes, stopping suddenly. Blowing her nose as she checked the money in her pocket. There was not enough for a room for the night in a hotel near Dorset Square, but there was probably enough, she thought, for a room closer to the railway station where she knew the hotels would be cheaper. The Marylebone Station area was within walking distance and she hoped she could use the hotel phone to try Lochy again. After sticking the key back under the mat for the neighbours, Rebecca left their flat and walked towards the Station area.

People stared at her. She noticed and wondered if they recognised her. She thought that perhaps, for some reason, her photo was in the news as a missing person. Passing groups seemed to drift by and her legs felt leaden as if trudging through deep snow. She could smell her own sweat and she seemed to ache everywhere as in a fever. She was more upset about Rosey, than she had felt about her uncle's untimely death. This troubled her, but then I hadn't seen his body, she realised. Rebecca only left these discomforting thoughts when she suddenly noticed; she had been walking around the perimeter of Dorset Square for some time and was now facing the wrong way.

***

Rebecca took a room in a Nuevo Hotel near Marylebone station. Signing in as Rosemary Gibbs. Well I might as well confuse the buggers if needs be, she thought. Basic facilities and no bath.

She showered immediately, letting the hot water spray across the back of her neck for ages, it was just wonderful. She thought of nothing, allowing the warmth to permeate her body, although it was still shaking as if cold. She was part and parcel of the gushing warm water, and she turned her face towards the shower head as if worshipping the sun, dreaming of happier times in California, hopefully cleansing all her troubles. Once she had washed and dried her hair, she felt so much better. Wiping condensation off the full-length mirror she looked at her naked body. Baby was beginning to show a slight swelling and her breasts were fuller. Squinting through her good eye, and putting her face closer to the mirror, she could see her swollen black eye was a real bruiser. No wonder people stared at me, no wonder, she thought. There was further amber bruising on her left shoulder and her ribs, probably from exiting the car.

In the last few years at her boarding school in southern England, (due to the possibility that Zak's vengeful influence was unlikely to extend across Le Manche) she was able to see her bone and vein structure clearly through her blue and mauve blotched skin, as she was then so anorexic. This was a period of paranoia tinged with acute anxiety and guilt. The recent years of therapy, and maturity, meant that she was fuller figured and only the sharply drawn white lines on her wrists were still visible as they stood out against her heated reddened skin, (forming a constant reminder of her despair at that time) although they almost disappeared as her skin cooled. However, she was still conscious of their presence, so continued to wear several bangles on both wrists, in public, as a reassuring cover to her past.

She wrapped her hair in a dry towel and slipped into the white hotel dressing gown and lay on the bed listening to the sounds of the city. So different to the sounds of Paris or Chicago, she ventured. She began to take stock of her situation. With clean hair and a decent pizza and coffee from room service she was thinking clearer.

Matthew is dead, uncle is dead too and I can't go to his funeral as I am supposed to be dead; and sweet Rosey is also. Which may have been suicide. She was too emotional, and I wasn't much of a flatmate as I was hardly there. She didn't just want someone to share the rent, she was looking for a companion.

I did neglect her though. Oh, guilt: guilt, fucking guilt. But suicide. Not Rose. You don't sell everything, all your worldly goods, even mine, eviscerate your whole domain and then top yourself. And who had just used the toilet? Bugger, my fingerprints are all over the flat. Then they should be I guess after all I did live there. Or maybe The Brethren thought that I had told Rosey Q was fake. Of course, they couldn't risk the possibility of anyone knowing. Damn, that means that Mel could be at risk. She had contact with Lochy and me, she knew we were involved in something important and time consuming, but then Mel had no idea really, although, they may think that she did, or that Lochy or I had told her. They couldn't risk that possibility either. I must see her tomorrow. She will know where he is. If she is alive? My God, baby, what an awful mess. I can't even find your father and he isn't aware of your existence and may well be pissed off when he finds out.

And They. Who are They? Professionals, according to the police. I don't see uncle's Christian Brethren as professional hitmen, although, considering the possibility, the Q scam has amassed a huge fortune, the Brethren could pay for professionals. Uncle said that there was enough revenue from the sales of the book of Q and the general Christian revival, to build three or four magnificent God Houses, as he calls them, and there would be enough money left to buy Jerusalem. When I gave Lochy this information, he said, *'that it was probably the only way 'your lot' would ever give it up'*, *Boom-Boom*. Dear Lochy, dear stupid Lochy, she thought.

With so much at stake, *they* wouldn't use a bunch of amateurs. Matthew's death was more professionally executed it would seem. Also, why the sham marriage between Lochlan and someone with my ID. I must see Mrs Wilson again. What did she say, 'there couldn't be two of you' after I told her I lived with Lochlan. However, obviously, there must be, and if I had died, then there would only be one. Only one Mrs Majewska from Illinois and Lochy would have his fortune and his 'false bit of stuff'; probably. Although he never seemed to be that sort of a bastard and I don't think I am that naïve; although I was totally with Zak I suppose. But, why Lochy's VW Marco? Why am I the owner, or is his wife? Unless of course… Exhausted, Rebecca fell asleep.

She hadn't slept well, the full force of Rosey's death and the vision of her swollen feet limpid in front of her pale insipid body kept forcing its presence, accompanied by a deafening blood rush in her head. Eventually she must have dozed as the early morning traffic roar awoke her and she burrowed under the covers for warmth. London may snooze, but never sleeps, she thought, but she was desperate for sleep. A sleep that never came as she kept seeing her parents, sat side by side in aircraft seats, holding hands as their plane fell out of the sky. She learnt, from the crash investigation there were two simultaneous explosions. *Boom-Boom,* and a sudden out-rush of air sucking everyone and everything into space. Passengers would have only a split second of realisation. Instant death in truth, and that was most comforting.

Rebecca fiddled absent-mindedly with her mother's wedding ring, and while one hand rested on her burgeoning tummy, the other reached up to lift her breasts and squeeze her nipples. They felt different, of course, as she was aware of these changes and was both excited and apprehensive in equal measure. My parents would have loved my Lochy, she speculated, and he would have adored them. She wondered why he only mentions his Mum, not his father. I must meet his mother, he visits her, so she can't live far away. I don't really know much about him, while he knows so much more about me. I seem to have told him everything, she thought, but then realised, compared to what Rosey had known, nearly everything Lochlan knew about her wasn't true.

She emerged from her bed and thoughts and showered once again, but took her time, more to use the facilities she had paid for up front, than her need. She dressed. Her underwear and slip had dried overnight on the radiator, which was the only reason to recommend the hotel, she thought, for without any ID reception took her cash for the room in advance. With her ever blackening eye and bruised cheek, reception was cautious. She didn't blame the bored receptionist for she knew it would have been hotel policy.

The cost of the room had left her with enough money to get through a few days, although, insufficient to book another room for the night. She had skipped breakfast as she still felt nauseous at times, although her morning sickness was easing, her nerves were as edgy and as wary as an urban fox, as someone had attempted to kill her, and had succeeded with Matthew, uncle Paul and Rosemary. Now clearly aware The Brethren's motto, *By All and Every Means,* meant anything was possible. She was scared, scared of everyone, and she knew, she must not communicate in any way, except orally, as she considered any use she made of technology would probably compromise her existence by indicating her whereabouts. The Bank of America needed her ID to regenerate her credit cards, but she couldn't flag up to anyone where she was. The police knew a Mrs Majewska was alive, but then, she reasoned, there must be two.

When Rebecca emerged from the stultifying heat of the hotel, she breathed in deeply. She had picked up a free tourist map from the hotel foyer and decided to walk to Hackney and visit the Orchid Restaurant as she was hoping to question Mel about the shut-down of Lochlan's Apartment, but mostly to talk to someone, just to talk to someone whom she felt would be discreet and understanding about her absolute terror of her and her baby's imminent death. She was reluctant to raise her profile until she had seen Lochlan.

It was still fairly early, but she had to be prudent with the remainder of Shaun's money and she thought the walk would do her, and the little one, a world of good. She took as many side streets as she could heading in her general direction, not entirely for stealth, but more often to avoid the traffic noise and pollution on the main roads. It was a fine day, with a cerulean blue sky, few clouds, and several silver aircraft that appeared to hover in their slow decent over London. She looked up and thought with much sadness. Only a few months ago I was up there in one of those gleaming planes, heading for Heathrow Airport, full of optimism for my future studies and looking forward to meeting uncle again.

***

Rebecca walked into a cemetery after a while to take a rest on a wooden seat, dedicated to a dead somebody, as she was finding the walk more tiring than expected. Absent-mindedly musing on the names and dates on the gravestones, (the beauty and warmth of the day having lightened her mood, although, of course, it could not ease her mortal fear.) she found herself idly thinking that maybe she would call junior after her dad's Christian name and, if *It* was definitely a he, a middle name after uncle, dear uncle Paul: he would like that she thought, feeling a little tearful and full of regrets for everything. One name that caught her eye on a headstone near the entrance was Emmanuel, she liked the sound of the word, the way it tripped off the tongue, and anyway she countenanced, Junior could still be Emmanuel if *It* is a girl after all.

There are so many unfamiliar names on these grave stones, she thought, the plethora of foreign names a testament to London's cosmopolitan past, with some burials much older than this country's colonisation of the America's, she realised. Such a tiny country is this UK and yet more than capable of setting its mycorrhiza to embrace, transform and exploit the globe. That's what Lochy found amazing, and he is right, she thought. So many secrets buried here, so many locked into the soil. So many tales untold, because their dead body was laid to rest before their nearest and dearest were buried next to or after them. So many not old enough to have outlasted their family and friends. Very few as old as the 'Orlando the Cat' lady, Kathleen Hale. Uncle was lucky the law on homosexuality changed in his lifetime; an acting career which led to him taking so many macho parts, including Heathcliff, to obfuscate his true nature. She noticed several graves carried inscriptions that said *Loving and Devoted Wife*, often under or after their husband's name. They cannot all have been devoted. And so many biblical references to Romans V1. Really? Then she read the inscription on her seat. *Peace: Out of Pain: at Last.* All at once, the reality of her present situation sank through her whole being, wondering if she would be able to tell anyone her story, before her demise. "*Age Quod Agis,*" she said out loud.

Rebecca was deep in these thoughts, when she was disturbed from her trance by a smartly dressed, suited, middle-aged man, whose coming she had not heard and who took a place on the long bench seat rather too close to her, turning a little towards her when crossing his legs. He had odd socks she noticed. It was evident from this obvious gesture that he wanted to engage her in conversation, producing, a salesman-contrived smile. He was obsequiously charming and evidently fawning his concern, while he tried to place her accent and elicit her name. He also asked her if she was the victim of domestic violence or needed help in any way, while seeming, at the same time, head bent forwards, to be looking at the reflection in his over-polished shoes, or staring at his exceptionally immaculate long fingernails, much longer than her own, she thought. She was suspicious and only uttered a few choice expletives in French as she wondered if he could possibly be tasked to kill her. She moved on abruptly after he placed his cold hand lightly on her thigh, feeling the sharp pressure of his nails.

She stood up straight away and resumed her walk, at some pace, without commenting, or glancing behind, heading past a long line of headstones and yew trees towards the far exit. The man followed; although somewhat nonchalantly and slowly. However, her pursuer would suddenly appear the other side of the many dense yew trees, that filled the grave yard, when she lost sight of him. Disturbed by her pursuer, and the realisation that he had been quickening his pace when unsighted by her. She began taking a random route through the maze of pathways between the gravestones, staying out of his sight line, worried that he may have a gun. Eventually she managed to join a solemn group of people at an internment and tried to hide behind a very large lady, standing close, to what appeared to be, (judging by its inflated size) her baby in a pushchair.

Several mourners stared at Rebecca, probably wondering to whom she may be related, but Rebecca thought they were staring at her inappropriate clothes, yellowing bruised face and swollen eye. She had to catch her breath when she realised, that within a few weeks, she could have one of those: an actual, needing to be fed, baby, or even, she thought, (joining the mourners in their solemnity) being lowered with due ceremony into a grave. What was it uncle Paul had said when he signed the legal papers that enabled his guardianship?

One will never truly gain adulthood Rebecca, I now realise, until one takes complete responsibility for someone you love, and hamsters don't count.

Then she realised, taking her away from her thoughts, she had been spotted by her polished pursuer and he was closing in on her by short-cutting over the graves and making rapid progress towards her, gesturing at times, or pointing in her direction. Could it be a gun? She wondered. Moving stealthily towards the exit, by walking briskly around the outside of the group of mourners, whose eyes followed her, and her potential assailant's progress. The vicar courageously continued his incantations, seemingly unperturbed.

Rebecca emerged from the cemetery gates onto the main road, at speed, bumping into the side of a parked car, startling the person sat in the driver's seat.

"Do you mind," he shouted as he 'buzzed' down the car window, "This is prime real estate."

"Sorry, sorry, I didn't mean to, I am being chased. Can I get in... please," The driver responded kindly to Rebecca.

"Yes, okay, get in. It's a real estate anyway," he said as he reached across to open the passenger door for her. She jumped in, breathing heavily.

"What's up my girl," he asked somewhat annoyed by the intrusion.

"There he is!" Rebecca exclaimed in a whisper.

Suddenly the driver flapped down the passenger sun visor and ordered her to freeze.

Her pursuer looked up and down the street for a while, even straying into some of the driveways of several houses that would have offered someone cover, but eventually he seemed to give up and walked back in through the cemetery gates. She started a move to get out of the car.

"Stay still," the driver said. "It's wise to stay still, people will only see us as the seat head restraints; and he may double back, an old pro trick." And he was right, as a few minutes later, the middle-aged man walked out of the gates and looked around, obviously expecting Rebecca to emerge from one of the house gardens of the long road. He stood right by their car, looking up and down the street, but eventually he moved off and back into the cemetery.

"Who is he?"

"My husband," Rebecca offered.

"Bit old for you, ain't he?"

"He hit me. He's violent, he thinks he owns me and watches my every move."

"Your face has certainly copped it. I hate men who hit women, they're cowards. You were lucky, he seemed determined to find you, although I make my living from people like him. People who want to find out what their other half is up to. Jealousy, that's what it's all about. Still, true love runs deep, as they say, jealousy is an inevitable consequence, and it's not just men who hire me, quite a number of women do as well, but the women seem to be disappointed if their husband; well, their men, are really up to nothing; actually playing golf or something, which is often the case, although the majority of women are cheating, so you think it should even out. One or two have even accused me of collusion."

She just sat there and listened. Although his facial expressions solicited conversation, she was too pensive and apprehensive about her situation.

"Thank you. You, saved me, thank you. Can you give me a lift? But I can't pay, he's got my money."

"You're welcome; you can't see through the windscreens of these estate cars, because the screens have an acute angle on this model, too much reflection. That's why we use them, can't see in, see."

"Are you a private detective?"

"That's what I was saying. I was to look out for someone who said that he was going to that funeral in there: did you know the deceased?" She shook her head. "Well he hasn't turned up so far: not the deceased, he's definitely turned up." She missed the joke as she was more fixated on getting a lift at any cost. "But I will have to wait, so I can't give you a lift I'm afraid. This is the third funeral he hasn't attended recently, so I think he's definitely for the chop."

"I would divorce him for a lack of imagination, myself."

"I'm sure you would, but a guy would be a nutter to cheat on a cracker like you. My name's Tom. Here, let me give you my business card, '*Tom's my name. Detection my aim*'. That's what it says on the back. You may need my services and I am known to be discreet and I'm reasonable."

"Thank you, Tom," she said as she took the card. "I can be most grateful, and I do owe you one, you saved me."

The detective was not sure what she meant, but he was hopeful, *most grateful*, meant much more. So, he reached over to lift-up the sun visor on her side of the car, getting closer to her than was necessary, deliberately brushing her breasts. She didn't flinch as she was as much flattered as desperate. Rebecca smiled at him. She wasn't getting out.

"I could give you a lift, if it's not far, if I can take it out of your expenses," he said this as he grinned at her, in the hope of eliciting more clarity.

Rebecca smiled at him again and acquiesced, she was tired and had been scared and just wanted to get far away from the guy in the cemetery. Walking was too risky. "I need to get to the Thai Orchid Restaurant in Hackney high street, I'm expected there at twelve." Rebecca thought it was prudent to let him know, someone was waiting for her at a specific place and time.

"That's not so far, I know that beat, grew up in the Tower Hamlets, didn't I, moved to Shoreditch, didn't we. Do you know it? Snobby area now, wife says it's come up because we moved in," he grinned at her looking for approval, as he drove on past the cemetery.

She let the detective talk as she was pleased to have a chance of the lift, as her bruised face and her back were paining.

"That's all you get in the end, a bit of this earth two by one metre and that's it. My missus and I have sorted our burial with the co-op, all paid up proper. We want an internment though, can't be doing with those little plaques that they put in the cemetery after the 'barbecue'. We want proper grave stones, 'cause it looks better, all those slabs of granite and marble yachting at differing angles across the lawns, angels at angles, my wife says, much more interesting than a flat lawn of tiles."

He reached into the car door pocket on his side and offered her a swig of Polish vodka, which she declined. Then he took a gulp, replacing the cap on the bottle skilfully with his teeth, something that has been well practised Rebecca surmised as he managed the whole operation at the traffic lights before they had even thought of changing. She let him ramble on excitedly, as men always do, she thought, when they think they may get some action.

"My Aunt Daisy, my Mum's sister, had one of those ethical burials after she was cremated, plonked the ash pot in a part of a woodland site, they did. Paid for it up front didn't she. Said she wanted daisies planted all around, but she hadn't read the small print had she, daisies were not allowed as they spread into other areas. Turned out that my mum had to plant primroses instead. Tried to get her name changed to Primrose, which Auntie wouldn't have minded, but they won't do it posthumously."

She laughed and said *Boom-Boom,* not really knowing why, but because Lochy always did. "I guess, Tom, when you consider all the gas used in the burning of a body, plus all the polluted smoke, it's probably more environmentally friendly to bury the body, anyway, compost the earth and push up the daises."

"Something left for the 'Time Team' as well... don't you think?"

She didn't answer, all this talk of death had quietened her mood and she was troubled about his true intentions, as she knew nothing about him, but she felt that she had no alternative.

Eventually he pulled off the Hackney road into an area that seemed to register with Rebecca as they turned in past the 'Maxi-Taxi' office housed under the first railway arch tunnel of many. The area appeared less sinister now as it was sunny broad daylight and many of the defunct small businesses were brightly coloured with large showy advertising posters flanking the railway line. Tom reversed his car expertly into an empty archway just a few tunnels down. He has obviously been here before she thought. The tunnel was much nearer to the main road than the archway of her near demise, and it appeared much darker in this tunnel with the one open end so bright. She bulked at its proximity to her ordeal, the coincidence was disturbing to her, as she began to think that all the, e*vents* (as Lochlan referred to recurring, disturbing, situations) had an inevitable outcome, orchestrated by an unseen hand, but she was past caring what may happen, having agreed to this by inference, if not explicitly, she figured she probably knew as much about Tom as she really knew about Lochy. With little money, she felt she had no alternative.

"Listen, my girl," he said as they pulled up. "I don't get as much fun as most of my clients, mores the pity: I'm giving you a lift in the hope that you could give me a big thank you with those red lips of yours and I don't mean a kiss, and I don't mean offence either. Do you understand?"

She heard the throbbing echo of the engine die, the clunk of the doors lock, the swish of a released seat belt and the buzz of a zipper. The private dick pulled out his penis, spit on his hands and wet the head. Finding herself in a similar situation in the Bois de Boulogne on many occasions she knew her best policy was to appear keen to oblige and do a 'good job', exiting with a smile as soon as possible, leaving a false phone number if a client asked for one; something all the girls did.

Rebecca released her seat belt and then her 'man'. She was practised and she was good, as deft as her detective was with the vodka bottle top; he was sweaty, but clean, she was relieved, as not all men are, and it was soon over. She withdrew and swallowed, whilst glancing up at his contorting face.

"Pass me the vodka please Dick." She wanted to say 'dick-head', but dared not, and took a gulp as a mouthwash, then passed it back, he took a swig.

"God you're good my girl and generous, no wonder your old man was after you."

"We best get going Tom, it's nearly noon," she said

***

Rebecca arrived at the Orchid, thirsty, tired and hungry. When she entered the restaurant, it was lunchtime. James the owner was there. This was unusual, although she had met him in this restaurant and another a few times. He owned several Thai restaurants in London, all called The Thai Orchid. Thai cuisine was her favourite food. Thailand was where she had always planned to take her honeymoon when she married Lochy; someday.

She sat on a sofa in the waiting area, helped herself to some water and James came from behind the bar and till and joined her.

"Hi, I haven't seen you for a while, how are you?"

"It's Rebecca, Professor Majewski's ere, well, ere, wife," she said, realising that James was floundering for her name.

"Yes. Rebecca: Sorry, I am hopeless at names as I meet so many people. Yes; I'd heard the Professor had married. Congratulations. What can we get you?"

"Is Mel about? I was hoping to see her."

"No, unfortunately, she has left and gone back to her village taking the best Thai chef in London with her. I thought that you would know."

"Oh dear! Was one of her children ill?"

"No, not at all, that kind husband of yours gave her a considerable sum of money, for services rendered, no doubt. Oh, sorry again, I meant severance pay. She and her husband are back in Thailand for good. I could have done with some more notice. I was a bit miffed I can tell you Rebecca as Brussels now tells us that we must employ a chef from the EU unless we can prove that a Thai chef from Thailand is essential, and that means paper work and time. What planet are they on? I can't wait to ditch the whole lot. And of course, your Professor hasn't deigned to come here since you have moved to *The Fine* Borough of Islington no less and right next door to the PM's post electoral mansion."

Upset by the information about Mel and Lochy, she was only listening to James with half an ear, especially as he talked so rapidly, she daren't interrupt. People thought that he was a regular coke user, but Lochy said that it was just his way. During his diatribe she indicated that she was moving to a table to eat and he sent a girl over to take her order. They knew each other from her previous visits. In answer to Rebecca's enquiry, she said that her Professor had indeed moved to a big house in Islington, just three blocks away and that Mel was very happy as back in her village she was very rich lady. Rebecca acknowledged that the waitress's reference to *blocks* deferred to her American accent, which was only slight due to her time at schools in Europe, but none the less, had been honed recently, by her two years at Berkeley California. *A time of little study, but many men, too many to mention*, as Lochy had informed the same waitress when they last ate at the restaurant. Was everything she had told him in confidence fair game? She had thought at the time. However, any protest was difficult, as she was feigning indifference, while Lochlan's sock-less foot was stroking her crutch under their restaurant table.

Berkeley wasn't exactly as Lochlan inferred, it was just that her time there coincided with the development of dating apps, and it was just so easy to connect with people, who were in general horny and just wanted casual sex. All ages and all interests; it was distracting and the first time in her life that she was living independently with an allowance from her parent's bequest. What was all that about? She asked herself, almost hoping for an answer, what was I doing at Berkeley? Swinging and grieving, I guess.

She ordered the set lunch as it was good value. The food was wonderful, and the wine had calmed her, she had to 'say' sorry again to baby. When Rebecca went to pay the bill, James the owner was behind the bar and 'on the till'. This was very unusual and in response to her enquiry, he said that he was short of staff.

"I need work James. I could do the till, I'm trustworthy. I need to earn some money, to hole up somewhere and collect my thoughts. Say yes."

"Gosh! You are desperate, I could use someone, especially evenings. It's only the minimum wage, plus all you can eat, but not drink mind you, alcohol that is. You could start now. I hate this till thing. Just a minute." She waited while he settled the bill of another customer and resumed. "When I saw the state of you, your cheek and that eye, I did wonder if things had gone awry between you and the prof, but I am not one to pry. It's going to take quite a bit of make-up. I will ask Nombel to tend to it and you better borrow some clothes from her or one of the other girls. Thank God. You are my saviour. I thought I would have to do tonight, and tonight is my squash night. You can have Mel's room for now, but the rent comes out of the wages." He charged her for her meal. She understood why he was a successful business man.

The lunches were nearly over, so she was able to rest in Mel and her husband's room. Her room now. It was small, but adequate. It must have been cramped for two and the kitchen and bathroom were shared. Her baby was objecting to the spicy food and possibly the wine and her feet ached, so she lay on the double bed which took up most of the room. Nombel said, the till operator's hours were from 12.00 noon until 2.30 pm, and from 6.30 until 12.30 am, depending on how long it took to cash up. Rebecca realised she would be able to seek out Lochy in the morning and this she resolved to do.

***

"Excuse me, may I ask what you are doing here? This is a private garden." A sprightly middle-aged women, who was being walked by an enormous Alsatian dog, had approached Rebecca in the garden that lay opposite a short terrace of large Regency town houses; of five floors, each having ornate cast iron railings to the fore-garden, with steps up to a large panelled impressive front door.

"Really, I am so sorry, it looked like a park and the gate was open."

"That's an oversight er, Miss?" her intonation implied a question, but her dog's alert presence implied an order. Still paranoid after her recent ordeal in the cemetery and wary of all strangers, she said the first name that came into her head.

"Gibbs."

"Now that is interesting: Miss?"

"Rosemary."

"Did you realise that you were staring at the properties across the road for more than half an hour: without moving may I add."

"Yes probably, I was waiting for someone to go in or come out of one of them."

"I see, a fan of the PM are we; or were you just waiting for someone to pop out and predict the weather?" The dog lay down as if he had realised, he was no longer on guard and yawned.

"You must be security madam, I'm sorry to have bothered you. I can see I was acting suspiciously."

"No, no, I am just one of the residence's neighbourhood watch team. Humphrey and I always walk here, don't we Humph?" The dog stood up as he recognised his name. "The PM's not here at the moment or else we would have made a citizen's arrest, wouldn't we Humph?" This was said with just a touch of irony and Rebecca thought, yes, I bet they would. Why take a dog for a walk in a small entirely fenced park garden and not let it off its lead if it wasn't fully trained to *attack and restrain* when released.

Leaving the private garden, she decided to walk around to the back of the terrace and try to see if she could discern anything of Lochy or his possessions. There were only eight houses which made up the Regency part of the terrace at the front and she knew Lochy now lived in one of them and she had already surmised that he must have received his payment to have leased such a

116

grand house, and, therefore, he possibly received his payment just after he married her substitute. She was also troubled as such pomposity didn't accord with the purchase of a VW Polo, or his dislike of *posh vehicles from Bavaria* as he referred to his new car.

She didn't know which house was his, but she thought, if she asked the question to the 'dog lady' she would arouse even more suspicion. When she was certain she intended to knock on the door and confront Lochy as she had given up on his phone having tried several calls to Lochlan's number on Nombel's cell phone, to no avail, and decided that she must be *persona non gratis.* Or should I knock? She wondered. He may just think I've disappeared. Or it may have been Lochy who had tried to kill me. Oh No! I can't go there; but maybe he was the professional. It was his VW after all. Oh! My God! No: don't go there. Anyway, his Mrs Majewska may even answer the door, what then. What if they had colluded to retain the whole payment for themselves? She considered cautiously.

At the rear of the terrace there was no clear view whatsoever of the back of the houses. What originally may have been coach houses and stables, had been converted into Mew's houses in different, pastel shades. Rebecca was rather taken by them as the coloured houses reminded her of seaside vacations with her parents in the town of Swanage, England. She almost smelt the sea. One was up for sale. She noted the telephone number and decided to contact the agent for a viewing. As she was running late for work, she caught the bus back to the Orchid.

She tried to phone Lochy once more, from the Orchid, but the line was still dead. She had also tried directory enquiries and researched on line from the restaurant, through his various publishers, even phoning them from The Orchid, using a pseudonym, but none of her efforts turned up a new number. Not only was she *persona non gratis*, but it would seem that he was also. She had also phoned Tony's office during her extensive enquiries and Rebecca booked into his clinic immediately for a check-up and a possible due date. Everything was fine with her baby. She was very relieved, and Tony had allayed her constant worry about possible brain damage to the baby due to her inhalation of carbon monoxide, as the incident had been several weeks before and she had not lost consciousness. She didn't mention the circumstances of course. Tony had attended her uncle Simon's funeral. Rebecca had assumed that he would and had her plausible excuse for her absence ready. Only twenty-three weeks to go, according to Tony, and he suggested that she should have the baby at his maternity clinic, which was at Henley and overlooked the Thames. She had been there before under different circumstances. Tony never mentioned her conditions to anyone, ever, including her parents, (with whom he had been acquainted through his practice) as confidentiality meant just that. Knowledge is power of course and he didn't come cheap, but he knew there was money in her extended family, so he could afford to be patient.

***

As Rebecca was now wage-earning, she took a taxi to her appointment with the estate agent handling the Mew's house, or Property Management Consultant as his business card read. When he asked the nature of her employment, she said she was an Ancillary Financial Consultant as opposed to till operative, which she hoped would sound as if she could afford the house. The exterior had some character, but the interior possessed no redeeming features. Left alone to wander outside the property to view the patio area, she walked up the alley-way to communal refuse bins. Unseen by the estate agent, she checked the alley-way gate, it was shut, but not locked. Inside, the property was modern and clean and light. She was only interested in the view over the back to the terrace gardens from the bedrooms. The agent was droning on about insulation and the solar panels and she had switched off, until she heard him say, the next house along from the PM, the one with the large conservatory, was occupied by Professor Majewski and his wife, and he had leased it to him.

"For how much?"

"I am not obliged to say Miss."

"Okay, I could look it up."

"Actually, it's not common knowledge Miss, we don't know why."

"Really." She wasn't surprised. Given the possibility of a devious payment to Lochlan by the Brethren. "For how much is this house advertised?"

"Two point Two million."

"For this little house, no! Then his house must have cost…"

"A small fortune Miss Stein."

"Crikey, the Professor has done well for himself. What number is it?"

"Twenty as I recall, yes. PM's twenty-one. It's the land Miss Stein, they have large gardens, especially for The City. You could get half a dozen houses of this size on there. Even if you knocked down the Majewski's house we would still be able sell the land for millions, depending on permissions. It's the land that's finite, you see, they're not 'making' anymore are they? Especially in London. All houses go down in value eventually of course."

"Do they?" Rebecca asked, unconvinced.

"Yes, always: they all deteriorate to dust in the end. The older they are the more they cost to maintain. I wouldn't have one for love or money and I wouldn't want to live next to himself with all that security next door. Look at all those bird boxes up in the trees in the PM's garden. Cameras everyone. You would need clearance if you wanted to buy this one."

"Yes, I suppose I would, as would the birds no doubt. Isn't that lady in number twenty naked? Who is she, the one in the conservatory, the one with bracelets and a choker?"

"That's Mrs Majewska, and they're not bracelets, they're tattoos."

"Really?"

"Yes, we drew lots to see who would get this assignment today." The agent started flushing and grinning inanely, shuffling on his feet.

"And you won, obviously. Is she always naked? It sounds like you expected her to be."

"Yes, she is, often naked, so my colleagues tell me, if they have been selling these Mews's."

"Oh, I see, she has lived here for a while then?"

"Yes, years before he moved in anyway."

Rebecca was finding all this information of confusing interest, having never even seen a photo of Dianne at Lochy's apartment, *out with the old and in with the new*, as he would say, her Tattooed body was a surprise. As was the possibility she had previously lived next to the PM for several years.

"How do you know they're tattoos? Have you seen her in the buff, up close?"

"Yes, through the binoculars: the ones we keep for prospective clients to view the roofs condition: tiles, guttering, stacks, you know!" His neck reddened and beads of sweat appeared on his brow as he said this.

"May I borrow them?"

"Well, yes, um, yes, okay. Just use the one lens, or you will exacerbate that eye of yours."

Adjusting the focus, she brought her rival clearly into view.

"Do you want to express an interest in this property, Miss, as I am all behind."

"So is she! But no thank you, I like the house, but not the view through the rear window."

The agent had the courtesy to give her a lift to the Orchid, which surprised her, as he never asked her why, or how she had taken a hit to the face. He had also noticed that she did not come by car, although that's not so surprising, she thought, as estate agents often judge a person's ability to afford a property from their clothes and mode of transport, but also, perhaps, from the size of the sapphire on her finger.

Rebecca was more than intrigued. Wracked with jealousy, with aching heart, seriously confused, down in the dumps, wanting answers, devoid of reason, not thinking clearly, and not seeing too well with her addled brain, painful cheek and one closed eye. She had to know, she had to know. Foolishly, she decided to return the next day and explore the gated alley-way.

She borrowed some small, but adequate binoculars dumped in the lost property drawer behind the bar. They lived amongst an assortment of jetsam, including; several keys, lighters, umbrellas, hand bags and a child's toy, but also, two bras, two jumpers, several scarves, one pair of red silk knickers, and a gun. A real one. A small hand gun, A .380 calibre Magnum pistol: loaded. She had checked and wiped her finger prints with the knickers. Well, she thought, you never know, by whom or where this gun may have been used. She felt that she had to tell James, the owner, so she phoned him, but he asked her to put the gun back in the lost property draw, because it was there, he said, because if the police found it, *We* could say, it was a recent lost property and *We* wouldn't be culpable. He liked to know that it was in the L.P.

drawer as it was reassuring. She decided not to ask any more questions, but she felt far from reassured, feeling much more vulnerable when cashing up.

***

In the early morning, after the usual kitchen routine and chit chat with her house-mates, she went back to the lost property drawer. She wanted to touch the gun again, she didn't know why, but it was a compulsion. Some strange connection to her Pa. When she was a young girl, she had often gone to the shooting range with her father, although her mother was not so keen on her shooting. Her dad had a few hand guns and one he used to wear about his person occasionally. He used to say, *Well this is Chicargee don't ya know,* mimicking Doris Day, when she asked him why he carried a gun.

Rebecca faltered as she recognised the silk knickers were most probably hers. The ones that she had lost several weeks ago as they, Lochy and her, celebrated the conclusion of the 'Q Project' with rather too much champagne. They had eaten together in the Orchid, and he had challenged her to come downstairs from the ladies wash-room in the restaurant *sans* underwear. She took them off and thought she had put them in her sling bag. From the position of their table she knew he would glance up her skirt as she descended, and that another diner had also looked up, although she didn't know who, but she was certain. Rebecca seemed to have a sixth sense and somehow knew instinctively when someone was ogling her rear. She then spent the rest of the evening opening her legs just enough to give Lochlan a furtive glimpse of her pussy, as he always called her sex, while later he had slipped off his flip flops and moistened his foot by engaging with her crotch under the table. They both showed great restraint at table level trying their best to appear normal diners; although eventually, her usual taciturn resolve dissolved into giggles in front of the waitress.

At the end of the evening, while climbing up the stairs to his apartment Lochlan stayed several steps below, looking up at her. She liked spending the evening teasing him by moving in an exaggerated suggestive way. She tucked up her skirt, just enough to show a little more of her cheeks. At the top of their stairs she was wet and ready for him and just before she had put the key in the door to enter the apartment... he had parted ... and entered her... pulling her skirt right up. He stood erect, moving slowly in and out...easy for a while... then suddenly banging her against the door: hard, holding firmly and roughly onto her hair. They had uncontrollable giggles and laughter when Mrs Wilson came out of her apartment to investigate; they slipped into their place and made love in the hall.

'Oh! Lochy where are you? What are you doing? What the hell's going on?' She thought sadly.

***

At midnight Rebecca had hailed a taxi and was back at the pastel coloured mews and easing open the gated entrance to the alley-way. This she had chosen to do against all logic driven solely by her confusion and a desperate need to know; to satisfy her curiosity. She also in some perverted way expected to be challenged by the PM's security personnel. This was a stupid idea. She should have known this, and probably did realise, somewhere deep in her thoughts, but she was desperate for answers, almost any answers, as it now seemed an age since her last clear memory of the meal in The Park Restaurant and her conversation with her late uncle. Since then there had been *nothing but events dear boy; events*. Lochy always said that phrase when things went wrong, mimicking a posh upper-class English accent, but she never understood why, and he never explained.

She didn't know exactly why she was there, she only knew her jealousy of Dianne was palpable. In her darkest dreams, she kept seeing a naked Dianne getting married to Lochlan. An 'Amazonian-women' standing next to a suited Lochlan, in a grand ceremony with her uncle Paul as best man. Even her own mother was there and seen taking off her own wedding ring and passing it to uncle Paul. At the various wedding scenes her brain conjured in her despair, her dad was nowhere to be seen. Other dreams sometimes involved death, often of herself, followed by her funeral and the mourning of Lochlan and all her family. Her dad was always there. Jealousy is a tangible force in many respects, certainly it motivates, but it is not a bedfellow with rationality.

Rebecca had eased open the alley gate and was looking through binoculars at the rear of no. 20. when she saw Lochy pass an upstairs window. It was late, but he was still up and about as usual. Transfixed, although the she had to position the lenses a little away from her black eye and swollen cheek, she was waiting for a view of her rival in name (and it would seem fortune) through the same window of the same upper room. If she was able to view them kissing or engaged in some intimacy, then she would know she was usurped and Lochy, contrary to all her intuition and her previous understanding, was a complete bastard, and may well have tried to kill her. She needed to know. She really needed to know. A light was on at the attic level, it went out simultaneously with the stream of water she heard cascade down a sewage pipe. Could Dianne live up there? She wondered.

Suddenly a light came on in the basement. She could just see the top third of the basement window; then a spread of light; followed by a head and eventually a full figure emerging up the basement steps to the garden level. The person was coming towards her carrying something. She had to move, she knew she had to hide. If it was Lochlan she realised that she couldn't explain her presence and if the person was security; likewise. Yet there was nowhere to move to. Nowhere. No hiding place from the all-pervading glare, no dark shadow in which to play dead, nothing. 'Jesus, fucking Jesus' she said to herself as she scampered up the side of one of the large refuge bins and using a foothold on an adjacent bin, flopped in, pulling down the lid behind her. She could hear the persons feet on the flagstones and as they came closer, there was a blaze of light, a thin strip along the warped edge of the bin, they were going to open her bin. She thought they were going to open her bin. They were. She pulled the neck of her jumper over her head, like a hood, and made herself small, bringing both her knees up to her chin, while shutting her mouth and eyes tightly as they threw their waste into her bin: closing the lid firmly.

Only then did she feel the damp ooze of kitchen scraps seep through her jeans. She could smell fish. Peeping and breathing through the warped edge alternatively; only when the automatic light went out, did she dare to try and lift the lid fully and climb out, but the lifting arm of the lid had clunked down firmly, the lid was locked. Push as she may hard against the lid with her shoulders and back, making a real effort, peddling hard in the ever-squidgy waste, she made no progress. Fucking hell, this is awful, what am I going to do? How stupid, acting like a love torn teenager, stupid, fucking maniacal. She chastised herself. Bugger.

She thought of rocking rhythmically to and fro to upset the bin in the hope that the impact would burst open the lid, attempting a side to side motion, jerking back and forwards, causing the bin to move, slowly drifting on its wheels. The wheel noise was deafening inside the bin and she was expecting Humphrey to start barking at any moment. She really didn't care who found her, even the big bad wolf. The air inside the bin was putrid and her rocking efforts seemed to have reduced what little air there was and she was gagging.

Eventually she calmed, she had to, just had to, as she was sweating and tired. Pressing her nose to the warped edge of the bin lid, she took long deep breaths of fresher air. She still felt like vomiting and eventually threw up inside the bin. As she was retching and expelling her guts, she thought she heard the noise of a vehicle reversing. Unmistakeably reversing; a large truck she thought, judging by the sound of the engine. Soon she was able to see the pulse of the orange reversing lights through the warped bin lid. Of course, she realised, it's a garbage truck, just like central Paris, they must collect the garbage in the middle of the night to avoid traffic congestion. Great, I will be rescued, she assumed, oh! sweet relief, I thought that I was going to die in here. Oh! Joy.

The Refuse truck came closer, she could hear the men singing as they worked along the Mews's coming ever closer. *We sailed on the good ship B, my grand papa and me, over the seven seas we did roam, we're working all day and we're working all night, we're so fed up we want to go home; we want to go home, we hate the foreman and we want to go home.* Such an appropriate song that she joined in the last line of the chorus and shouted help as loud as she could. She just wanted out of there. But no one seemed to hear her over the rattle and clank of the crushing machine, the singing, and the rumble of the pushed along bins. "Help!" she shouted as she banged fiercely on the lid of her bin, "help! help! help! me, I don't want us to die."

At that moment the lid was opened by one of the men.

"Jesus Christ!" he exclaimed as a young person of the female gender emerged from and with the contents of the bin.

"Over here!" he shouted to his mates, "we've copped another fucking immigrant."

The men helped her out of the bin and brushed her down with their gloved hands and then gave her a hand brush so she could finish the job herself, *on the bits that wobble* as one bin man put it to her. All the time this was happening she was crying, not just tears, but whimpering like a wounded dog.

"Are you English? Speak English?" the foreman asked.

"Yeah," she sniffled, "I am an American."

"That will have to do," he said. "We can't hang about here dealing with the authorities and all, we have a schedule to keep. Next-time, choose a landfill bin and sleep inside a plastic bag like the others do and fix a bit of twine to the handle so you can pull it open or you will end up in the crusher and you won't be the first neither my love. Here." He handed Rebecca some bottled water and having told her to keep it, they moved off. She was most grateful for the water, and drank all of it, a half-litre, without catching her breath. She was an emotional wreck. She had encountered the green-eyed monster before and she had done some stupid things in its verdant glow, 'but this begs the bagel' as her dad would say.

When she was staying in student halls at Berkeley, she had listened to the sounds emanating from the room next to hers, by putting a glass tumbler to her ear, and pressing it to the partition wall. She was snooping, because she thought Thomas was having it off with her room-mate, Marianne. Every time her room-mate went next door, she listened, feeling a jealous sickness welling in her stomach. Almost deliberately punishing herself as she heard her friend's sensual moaning. She was very taken with her and they had become close friends, as her room-mate was a good listener and recognised Rebecca's need to sound off about her parent's tragic death and her time in Zak's Parisian gang, to exorcise her still tangible grief. And to some extent her disbelief; that it was her life. Talking it through with Marianne helped. *Synaesthesia* her therapist said.

A year later, when their paths crossed at a mutually beneficial seminar, she was able to talk to her ex room-mate without malice. But it felt different. The feeling was stronger. With Lochy, the green-eyed monster was evergreen. Why? She couldn't say, but her love for Lochy was different. Maybe I had wanted his baby, she considered, or perhaps a baby. I had given having a child more than a passing thought lately, prior to realising that I was expecting, and it was always Rosey's and Marianne's chosen topic. Well; my chosen topic, I suppose. It must have happened the very first time Lochy and I made love. The very first time. We must be meant for each other, we must be, she concluded.

Rebecca soon realised she had been stupid. I have been running on the emotional adrenalin and surging hormones of early pregnancy, during a period of intense fear and anxiety and neither can be conducive to rational thought. What was I thinking? I could have been killed, crushed in the refuse truck and spat out the other end into landfill. I will walk the main roads back to the Orchid, as it should be safer and I'll try to hail a cab, she decided. Naturally, she knew all manner of weirdos and misfits come out at night in a City; after all, hadn't she been one of a group of defunct Parisian night owl's in a past life. A taxi did stop, but it had a passenger who wanted to share the fare to some place that she didn't recognise in the Hamlets, so she refused. The other taxis that passed in her direction were taken. She was bursting for a wee and had been holding on for the past few hundred meters, filling her head with these thoughts to desperately take her mind off her need, but eventually, when she was almost at the Orchid, she had to pull down her jeans in a shop door recess and crouching with her body side onto any passer-by, at last; release. She exclaimed, the relief was glorious, although, Rebecca was surprised how hot her pee felt and she never expected her piss to steam so much in the cool night air. Embarrassed, (as an orange coloured night coach full of staring heads passed bye) she decided to run the last few hundred metres and made it to the Orchid.

***

Professor Lochlan was a troubled man, traumatised with anguish, and thoroughly depressed. Everything had happened so swiftly, suddenly he was living in a very large sterile house with his whole life in packing cases, which he had no desire to open, as their contents would have revealed his previous life, a life that he now realised was infinitely preferable in every way to his present one.

The moment his illustrious next-door neighbour had thanked him for his competent endorsement of Q, Lochlan knew immediately, without a shadow of doubt, that he was undone; completely scuppered. The realisation he was a security risk, as the PM had inferred, dealt Lochlan, an unprecedented blow, when he realised he was effectively under house arrest.

At first, an invitation to drinks with the PM so soon after he moved in filled him with excitement and an unwarranted sense of self-importance. He felt he was moving up in the world; that he amounted to something. Lochlan had understood from the outset, that when The Project was concluded satisfactorily, he would meet a *VIP, A Dignitary,* as Bishop Frankford had put it, who was also aware of Q and all its implications. He certainly did not expect it to be a senior politician who had recently converted to Catholicism. Wondering why his good neighbour had converted, he was troubled when the PM said, jokingly, that he realised, after endorsing The Project, he may be answerable, eventually, to an even higher authority.

Lochlan understood the house purchase and sham marriage were planned well in advance in order to facilitate Rabbi Simon Cohen's Will and Testament. He was expecting some payment in shares via some convoluted method for his time, effort and authentication, but he wasn't expecting to have to marry anybody, let alone Rebecca. (A payment for *his* services rendered to his *wife* from her guardian, Simon, without any comeback to The Christian Brethren or his illustrious neighbour.) He realised Rabbi Simon's, relentless, persistent badgering, was to pressurise him to marry his niece, because any form of payment via her uncle, would seem completely legit.

Lochlan hadn't known that Rebecca and Simon were related until the marriage proposal was mooted. He had assumed, from the outset that Rabbi Simon Cohen was credible, and he still believed this to be true. He also understood the Brethren's need to keep everything 'in-house' and accepted the explanation for Rebecca and Rabbi Simon's apparent collusion and subterfuge. Once he had understood their relationship, he began to question the whole Project and his own contribution. Although he, Lochlan, was lead to understand, that Simon was the brother of Rebecca's mother, maiden name Cohen. He was reassured, however by Rabbi Simon Cohen's insistence that his niece had expected to meet him, Simon, not Lochlan, in the Thai Orchid after their first discussion about Q, and it was therefore coincidental, as she would have missed Lochlan, if he hadn't chosen to stay there for a few beers and to read. He wanted to believe him, but, remained dubious. After all, he thought, I did take her on a pub crawl to get her drunk and seduce her after my second meeting with Cohen in the biker's café. He began to realise, however, that there was the possibility Cohen's niece had been *introduced* to facilitate the method of payment from The Brethren.

Despite his reservations, Lochlan was still convinced their Project was wholly legitimate, because they were holy, God fearing men. He therefore suggested to uncle Simon Cohen, that as long as the passport was Rebecca's and the paper work was in place, he could marry anyone who looked vaguely like his niece, as you could find any number of women in Hackney who would take up the subterfuge for not an awful lot of money, depending on their habit. He certainly didn't want it to be Cohen's niece who would end up with a legitimate claim to half the money for mostly sitting on his face.

Simon Cohen's house in St Johns Wood and his sizeable, but not over impressive bank savings had been left to Peter his secretary and partner. However, his shares in a multinational company had been left to, his niece, on her marriage to Professor Lochlan Majewski. The investment was substantial and the dividend, even in a poor years trading, would provide a considerable annual income. The terms of her inheritance also stipulated that Rebecca and Lochlan reside as a married couple at number 20 Islington Park Gardens. Lochlan's present Islington address, or shall we say the lease was purchased for him and his *wife* from the sale of a few thousand shares. Who would have thought of buying shares in Microsoft in 1985 at their I.P.O. (Microsoft's first share offer) Not Uncle Paul Smith (aka: Rabbi Simon Cohen) you can be sure, but it did appear (to anyone asking questions) his extraordinary wealth had been due to an early and fortuitous, investment.

Lochlan had not slept well ever since Rebecca went missing. Hypnos was off duty and he was gambling too much, too often.

He had heard from Dianne that Rebecca's uncle had died while jogging in Regents Park and he was not at all surprised, as he always seemed overweight, breathless and flushed, whenever they met. He was also told by Dianne, her partner, (as she referred to Matthew) had died in a motorbike accident. Lochlan hadn't registered any emotion or regret in Dianne's loss and he made no connection between the two fatalities, he just felt sorry for all concerned, as he had assumed, (having had no communication from Rebecca) that she may be feeling abandoned by his sudden departure and excommunication from society. Although Dianne had said there had been no reports of *accidental deaths* in the London papers, but they rarely are, he thought, people fall underneath 'Tube' trains every week, (deliberately planned or suddenly, spontaneously, on a whim, when they just can't face another commute) but go unreported. He also suspected that she may be under house arrest as well, or maybe, that if she had found out that he was married, she just took off somewhere. He knew she hadn't gone back to the States, or anywhere outside the UK as he had her passport. He considered, that maybe, he missed her because he was spending too much time on his own. I do miss her conversation and laughter though, he thought.

His minder was Dianne. Dianne Mayhew-Robinson, his ex, although, she had only lived with him for few weeks (but not on the weekends) at his Park View apartment in Hackney, he was soon sure that was long enough and always looked forward to the weekends. Her fitness regime was punishing, and she was always up so early mornings and he was by nature a night owl. Even the head of faculty, Summerskill, had recognised this and timetabled most of his, Lochlan's, lectures in the afternoons, when his delivery was considered, by senior staff, to be less laconic. He was fascinated at first by a tall-fit-blue-eyed-blonde-tattooed-female-biker. With more piercings than a colander. But he soon found reasons not to be cheerful, as she had her own vegan dietary concerns which meant he often dined alone. Dianne at midday and he in the evening, late evening often.

She enjoyed posing naked, and frequently persuaded Lochlan to take photographs, with her camera, of her athleticism. Although, after the initial excitement, he was bored. She did sleep with him. Occasionally, reaching over his body to give him hand relief, especially in the mornings, before she went to shower.

However, she seemed to only want it that way. With her body curled up to his back, while pressing and rubbing her rings, it was almost as if she and he were one body. Dianne's obvious excitement increased as he reached climax. She told him that she liked to feel that his protuberance was hers. That's what she called his penis, a protuberance. He laughed at this, but quietened, when she reminded Lochlan that he called his penis 'Percy' and always said 'he was off to point Percy at the porcelain', whenever he went for a pee. Anyway, being prone to stomach upsets he was sure he was getting metal poisoning. He was quite happy to see her *ride pillion* with the late Matthew Reynolds. At least they could compare tattoos and chain mail, he thought. Lochlan almost faints if he has an inoculation.

He wanted to scour London, the country, do anything. Anything, but stay put. He had pleaded with Dianne that he was not a security risk; but she wouldn't listen. She said it was her job to keep an eye on him, as the book of Q had gone viral and the various threats to his well-being on social media were taken seriously by her bosses. He had been skulking in his room for the past few weeks, and he was going stir crazy, sleeping in his room with the packing cases that contained his library and all his accumulated paraphernalia, there was just room for a bed. It wasn't solitary confinement, as after all there was Dianne, and any number of television channels, although he mainly tuned in to the horse racing.

Lochlan often walked around the private garden, giving more than a passing thought to absconding, although he was rather scared of the large German Shepherd dog that was frequently walked at the same time by a neighbour, who often acknowledged him from a distance with a friendly nod or a wave. He was also troubled by the number of bird boxes in the parkland trees as Dianne had said they were cameras.

He was given only twenty-four hours to vacate his apartment in response to the death threats and he realised in hindsight, Dianne was a plant by the Brethren, or those acting for them. Dianne told him, at their wedding deception, she had introduced herself as a 'journalist' to ascertain if he had any devious attributes or unsavoury interests that might compromise an Amber-project if his discretions came out in public. Such 'things' that might undermine or besmirch his credibility, and therefore, the internationally understood value of his contribution. She had no choice, as an Amber-project is near compulsory in its importance. He thought it made good sense, as he clearly understood the procedure, (with some enquiries possibly discrete) when a potential replacement University Dean is considered. And Dianne comprehended the need for her journalistic role, once Q had been published, (and verified by him) and apologised for her deception. Advising Lochlan, although at the time she was reluctant to marry him, it was a Red-assignment.

Lochlan only realised this when he returned to collect a few remaining items, including his flattened beer can collection, and found the whole of his Park View apartment was being *swept* and steam cleaned to remove all fingerprints. Even the door-locks were being changed by locksmiths when he entered the communal hallway and he had never seen the stairway so clean. Although he thought it was excessive, he realised, *They* had to use all means possible to keep The Project secret. After all he ventured, although I understand I have been entrapped by Dianne, Cohen and his niece to augment and protect The Project; the whole Project has enhanced my reputation and endorsed my early proposition that Q must have existed.

Lochlan considered his situation. Hindsight, hindsight, hindsight. Who needs three wishes from the Djinn Genie, just one; hindsight; that would do me, he thought, in hindsight, I wouldn't have got myself into this mess, my individual freedom is worth more to me than any notoriety, ego bloody ego; stupid trumped up arrogance, how my other neighbour, the PM puts up with the entourage that mirrors his every move I will never know, but when pride pulls you in, you're in, hook line and sinker. And in hindsight, he considered, until I lost Becky, I just didn't know what I had, or could have had, or may have had. It was like shooting a beautiful creature; dead and finding out later it was the very last of its species. I never thought that I would miss her so much, and it's just not the sex, he told himself; okay, it was compulsive, and I do miss it, but I miss her raucous laughter even more, well at least as much. Bollocks, I am buggered, well and truly, and I'm technically married to her. I'm married to the woman with whom I'm in love and she doesn't know it; if she's alive; and I am a widower if she isn't.

***

Rebecca realised as she ran towards the Orchid, that it may be shut. It was well past two in the morning and only a few crotchety urban crows were cranking. The side door was dead-locked and although she had a key, she knew from experience that the door to the accommodation was sometimes double bolted. It was. She was usually in bed before the kitchen staff had finished the clearing and preparation for the next day's meals. Only Kukrit would be up early for the market, but she could not wait till 5 am as she was getting cold, the temperature had really dropped and the damp in her clothes exacerbated the situation. She wondered what she should do? I can't wake them now, not this late. 'I will go and see Shaun, he may be there, he seemed to be on his own, there was no obvious feminine presence and it is quite close', walking at speed to keep warm, there was intermit-tent traffic and the night air was dead-still, making sounds rever-berate off the tarmac as if near calm water. She heard a group of young men coming towards her, they were drunk, loud, compet-itive in their ribaldry and about 500 meters away. She felt wretched and stank of urine, fish, rotting vegetable matter and she was scared. She crossed the road to avoid them, not at her recent pace, but slower, much slower, falsely trying to exude a nonchalant confidence in the manner of the street wise. But they had seen her and when they realised that she was making for the pavement opposite to them, all the gang moved over to the same side of the road to face her. Someone shouted out.

"Show us your tits darling," and another stopped in the road not more than a spit away, and pulling down his jeans as he bent over, showed her his hairy bum and testicles. They all laughed. One of them poured some beer out of their beer-can onto his mate's bare ass and the recipient tried hoicking up his jeans at the same time as trying to run and give chase to his mate, who was running away laughing. Someone threw an empty beer can at the absconder and it clattered down the road as a passing taxi driver beeped the horn in a warning, scattering roosting pigeons.

She was scared, in fact terrified, and held her hand to her head as if she was holding a cell phone to her ear pretending to chat so that the youths would realise a listening witness and pos-sibly the police were only a call away, but to no avail, they jostled

132

her, one put his hand up her jumper and clumsily pushed up her bra, just as another yob was trying to pull down her jeans from the rear, forcing his hand around to the front and pushed his thumb into her vagina. The tallest tried to kiss her.

"Fucking hell! She stinks!" the 'kisser' exclaimed, and they all pulled away at the same time as he made as if to gag. "Jesus Christ, she stinks of fish."

"Don't let Donker shag her," another shouted, "You don't know where she's been." And they all laughed.

"She's probably already *been* in her fucking pants," another said as they all moved off, laughing and jeering.

Rebecca resumed her pacey walk immediately, although she could feel her heart racing, and crossed back over to Shaun's Café side of the road. She was absolutely terrified during her encounter with the youths; petrified, as so many perceived outcomes flashed through her mind. The incident had been so brief, but to her, it had seemed to be in slow motion. Although, she had not uttered a word, not a single word; instinctively. One word out of place could have resulted in a beating or rape or both. She had learnt this indelible lesson while she was living with bisexual, bipolar Zak. After one savage beating, it was bye-bye Zak. Thanks to uncle Paul's timely intervention.

She was moving at a jogging pace and nipped into the alley next to Shaun's Café, just as a police patrol car cruised past, she just hoped, she wasn't seen. After all she was supposed to be dead and the scam was so universally accepted, that her fear and paranoia considered the possibility, *By All and Every Means,* may also infer, even the police could be in collusion, as previously the welfare officer seemed to have been. She leant against the alley wall to adjust her bra and pants. As she tried to zip up her jeans, she noticed her zip was broken. She flattened herself against the wall and tried to calm herself by slow deep breathing, thankful she got lucky. She could only remember the 'kisser's' pallid face, neck tattoos, eyebrow studs, and the all prevailing malevolent smell of alcohol.

***

Rebecca rapped on Shaun's door with quiet taps of the door knocker. There was no answer. Now she had stopped moving she felt cold, famished and thirsty. Tension thoroughly dries the mouth and she was understandably extremely tense and very weak. What if he is with someone? she wondered. What if he is away with the Harriers? She knocked again, louder, but also louder than she intended.

"Who is it?" a voice asked in a soft Irish brogue.

"It's me Shaun. Rebecca."

"Just a minute."

When he came to the door in his 'boxer' shorts, his body filled the frame. She was unable to see past him to check if there was anyone else in the room.

"Will you look at yourself," he said. "You're not looking a picture." And invited her in, sensing that he 'owed her'. He was alone.

She flopped into the arm chair and he offered her a brandy, which she refused (and which he insisted that she drank, before she told her story.) She felt the warm glow of the liquid slowly pass around her body and she began to relax. He made them strong tea and toast, while she tried to remove her clothes in the tiny bathroom. (It had been built in an under-stairs cupboard and contained a short bath and a mixer shower which could only be used when seated.) In modesty she had tried to take off her clothes whilst crouching hunched over in the bath, with the door closed, but it was impossible. Eventually she stepped into the main room and just took them all off in full view of the kitchen and Shaun, although he only had a back view.

"How on earth do you manage in there, Shaun?"

"I don't, I use my gym for a full on, that's only good for a wipe and a whistle."

"Still it's on suite."

"You don't say? So is the kitchen and the back door."

She left her clothes in a heap outside the bathroom and leaving the door half open, washed herself down while she told him her lies to explain her predicament. She left out anything to do with Lochy or her midnight visit to his Islington house, and lied, telling him she had been locked out of the Orchid restaurant after a party. However, she did tell him the true story of her harassment by the drunk youthful gang. He said he was willing to get dressed and go get them. He thought her decision to escape by jumping into a wheelie bin was clear thinking. Sitting naked on the edge of the bath with the door open, drying her hair with a hand-held blower, and with a towel across her lap, she felt comfortable and safe with Shaun. It was the first time she had had Marmite. She loved it. Toast had never tasted better. Tea never more welcome.

When the treats were finished, he gave her a clean London Irish rugby shirt that was huge on her (he had explained that it was the rugby team for whom he played as a prop forward). She didn't know anything about rugby, but as she put the shirt on, Rebecca asked if he had a spare room. Shaun shrugged his shoulders and walked her to his only other room, he opened the door. The room was full. It contained three immaculate, highly polished motorbikes, gleaming like jewels.

"That one's called The Duke, as it's a Duccatti, the middle one's vintage, well; veteran, it's a Norton Dominator, that was my dad's and this one is my Harley, it's a Destroyer, called Thor. I did all the crank case engraving inside prison in my last year; an open prison. My mates brought the bits in."

"It's truly beautiful."

"Not as beautiful as you."

"Thanks, but I am not sure if that's a compliment," as she said this jokingly, she placed the flat of her hand on his shoulder, and he slipped his arm around her waist. Grouped as they were, in the doorway they could have been appreciating a spectacular sunset together.

"We will both have to sleep on the bed, although I could sleep in the armchair, but it's bloody uncomfortable. If you don't mind? The bed's a double, but it's only just right for a man of my size so we will have to get close. It will be alright, I will have to get up in a few hours to do the breakfasts, then you can sleep on. You have a nice figure, nice breasts."

"Thanks, Shaun. I'm pregnant."

"O'ere! You are having a bad time."

"The understatement of the year. I am fair pooped."

"Borrow my tooth brush and come to bed."

"No. I just couldn't. Use your tooth brush I mean."

"Here, chew some of my gum then, your breath pongs?"

"Thanks," she said. She liked the matter of fact way he told her.

***

They both fell asleep immediately. Although she was eventually awakened by a loud, deep, noise, not unlike the sound and rhythm of waves on shingle. Comforting at first, but which Rebecca would later refer to at her Trial *as like sleeping in the engine room of the Titanic.*

On opening her eyes his profile and his numerous tattoos were illuminated by the soft dawn light that filtered through the thin curtains. The hollow in the middle of the bed had thrown them together and she had instinctively snuggled up to his massive chest. She could see its rise and fall, and from her viewpoint it was like looking up the side of a hill, in part covered by the entwined tail of a tattooed griffin that disappeared into his chest hair. He was lying on his back and he had already told her the hollow in the centre of the bed was caused by his preferred sleeping position. He also said he snored, and he hoped he wouldn't disturb her.

She had slept for only two hours or a little more, maybe, and was annoyed to find herself awake, possibly because she had become conscious of his presence. Not just his snore, but his smell also. Her face was close to his upper arm, as big as her thighs, she thought. A complete tropical scene snaked around his biceps complete with palm trees, disguising, she ventured, a zig-zag of lightening that pierced a heart, which was underscored with the barely discernible lettering that read: *Mavis Forever.*

She lifted her knee to raise the duvet and looked down the length of his body, he was all muscle like a prize bull. She had been so disoriented by her disastrous few days that she hadn't looked at him or anything or anybody, including Rosey, in any detail. She knew he was taller than her by a good margin, but that he was so muscular, tattooed and hairy, she had not realised. However, she was beginning to notice his breathing had changed to something lighter and calmer, more of a nasal drone. She was about to lower the duvet in case she had disturbed him, when she noticed his flaccid penis was beginning to move, very slowly. It enlarged and rolled towards her across his lower belly. Too curious, she continued to watch as it extricated itself from his pubic and stomach hair by degrees until it stood fully engorged, erect and twitching. She listened to his breathing carefully, he didn't seem to be awake. She wanted to touch it with a similar compulsion to her need to touch the gun in the lost property draw at the Orchid Restaurant.

She had elegant hands with very long fingers. It was the reason that her mother had hoped she would follow her own concert career and set Rebecca, (from an age when she could walk under her mother's grand piano without stooping), to any number of frustrating piano lessons to her constant chagrin. Boarding school was initially seen by her as an escape.

As she wrapped her hand around his shaft, she knew he was a *big boy*, not so evident when seen against his large body. She had known many men and still she was captivated by this process. Shaun's development reminded Rebecca of her horse-riding weekends in Fontainebleau when she would be given the task of oiling the horse's hooves whilst the head girl held the reins. The smell of the oil, or something, always aroused the stallions and she would joy to watch their 'manhood' grow. Sometimes the girls would dare her to touch and when she did, the horse's member would twitch, like Shaun's, and she would let go laughing. She missed riding out. They were happy times. *The last time that a woman may have a male between her thighs that she can control.* Miss Greer famously said. Rebecca wasn't so sure, this was not true of her experience of 'riding' men.

With a shrill persistent ringing, Shaun's alarm broke through her distracted mood. He shot up, jumped out of the bed and while fumbling for the off button, he suddenly realised Rebecca was in his bed and he was stood there in front of her, naked and erect. Although swiftly declining.

"Sorry about that, my love," Shaun said apologetically. "That often happens in the morning, trouble is I can never remember what I was dreaming of." They laughed. "We call it the Ian Drury effect. You know, in his song, *wake up and make love to me.*" She hadn't a clue what song he meant, but nodded.

Shaun went through his early morning routine on remote. He had set out his fresh work clothes the night before as he did every evening after he had thrown his previous clothes in the wash and tumble dry. He did the same with Rebecca's clothes pile and told her they would be ready to wear by ten a.m. and he would bring her some breakfast at nine. Then he went through to his Café to open the doors. Rebecca took off Shaun's rugby shirt and snuggled down naked into the warm hollow centre of his bed. It had been several days since she had pleasured herself and she was a little sore from her rough handling, yet once again no matter what fantasy set her going it was always something to do with Lochy that finally brought her off. Her desire was more comforting than needy; and she soon slept soundly.

***

Rebecca was conscious of someone stroking her hair, and gradually bringing her up from her slumbering depths to be greeted by the smell of fresh ground coffee, a pain chocolate and Shaun. She sat up, ran her fingers through her hair, shook her head violently, and took a sip.

"Proper coffee, I didn't have that before."

"And good morning Shaun, how are we today? Did you sleep well? Would be a nicer greeting than your criticism of the house brew."

"Sorry. I was just so pleased, and pain chocolate. How did you know?"

"Believe it or not, some of the locals prefer NesCafé and a piece of toast, there's no accounting for it."

"That's maybe why they want to leave the EU Shaun."

"You may be right."

"This is so good, thanks. Thanks for everything. I won't bother you any more, when my clothes are done, I will be out of here. I live and work at the Thai Orchid. I was locked out last night."

"I know, you told me last night remember. But you're welcome."

He was sitting on the edge of the double bed, but near her. On impulse, she leant forward and kissed him, kissed him lightly, just brushing his lips; then she felt his large hand hold the back of her head in a firm grip and pulling her head towards him his lips melted into her mouth and she took him in, freely, all tongue and moisture and the taste of caffeine. His hands, their hands were everywhere, and Shaun had his way with her. Nothing was planned, by either party, it just happened, no one was more surprised than they were.

As she lay under the heavy weight of his body, just resting, feeling used, (yes used), but not abused. She felt more possessed. She understood that Shaun had taken her, quickly, roughly, and with great urgency. And she loved every moment. He remained in her, flaccid, for some time. Rebecca had wrapped her legs around his thighs, keeping him there, as she still needed to feel connected.

Eventually, he pulled out and rolled off and lay on his back and she instinctively snuggled up close and lay her head on his shoulder, slipping a hand up his T shirt and stroking his chest hair. A warm glow effused her whole being. They lay together close, for several minutes, each having entirely different thoughts. Her face was paining, as his strong kissing and rough beard had tortured her damaged face.

"Thanks," Shaun said. "It's been a long time, since; you know."

"Don't say anything, please."

"I should have taken precautions."

"I'm pregnant, silly."

"Oh, yeah, so you are." He blushed, which she found endearing. "I'm tied up here today, but could we meet this evening?"

"I am working this evening, but I could pop along about three. I would like that."

"Okay, pop in the café for a coffee this afternoon." She raised her eyebrows and looked up at him. "A *proper* coffee, okay. About three, it's not so busy then. There are more than a few things about you that I find intriguing."

***

As Rebecca walked to the Continental Café to see Shaun, she was feeling good about him, although the throbbing pain in her cheek had been exacerbated by their kissing; in truth, she felt as if she had been in a rugby scrum and been taken out by the prop forward, or should that be the forward prop? She could still feel a warm glow within and for the first time for days she started to notice things. Everyday things. The buses, the trees, the people; realising that she had been severely traumatised and just focused on her immediate needs; ever since she was disturbed in the fume filled car. Understandably, she thought, as she knew she should be dead, and must continue to remain dead. And if found, would be. She was certain of that now.

The money from her work at the Orchid was enough for her day to day expenses, as she ate there and had become fond of her little room and found the Thai girls and boys' company a welcome distraction. Some were older than her, but their attitude was so innocent at times and unworldly, it was like being with teenagers and such a contrast to her own anxieties. She was unable to ask anyone in authority for help, but she did feel the need to confide in someone. It now seemed more sensible to find out more about Lochy's situation. She wondered why she wasn't elated to find him alive, but then logic had told her that he must be. His death would have made headlines, the police would have told her, and even Mrs Williams or James would have known and said something. She was relieved, although, perplexed and quite overcome with jealousy when she saw him at the window of his new house. She resolved to find out more about Dianne, after all I supplemented her by design not desire, she speculated, and without Matthews intervention Lochy may well have stayed with her and may well have married her. Although, Lochlan had told Rebecca that any marriage was just a piece of paper of no apparent value, and its true value would eventually cost most men, half a house. She wasn't at all sure what he meant. Maybe, she considered, maybe, he was just using me like all the others. She understood she needed more answers, before she could confront him, as she had come to realise, her feelings were not based on the little she knew about him, but on an instinctive sensual connection. Lust, rather than fact. She considered giving Tom the detective a call, but in the end, she decided against the idea as Rebecca felt that he would be too curious and expect favours. She really hoped Shaun might help in some way. She obviously couldn't tell him very much, but she fancied, she might convince him her life was threatened.

***

Rebecca noticed Shaun's Café was called The Continental, and realised it was the same one she had seen, when Lochy whistled for her to cross the road after his second meeting with her uncle. She had not noticed this a few days ago when she had scoffed the 'All Day Breakfast' and endured the awful coffee. Although she was aware that something had registered on her periphery. They even sat at the same table. She was unable to understand how she could have had such tunnel vision at the time.

"No wonder you thought I was a crack-head Shaun, I must have looked a mess, I wasn't myself."

"You did look like a bag of shit and you spent ages staring into your coffee shaking your head. I took you for someone waiting for a trick and going turkey. I knew your diamond ring was worth something and you don't get a tan like yours in the UK, so I expected you to pay. I didn't think you would run, I usually spot the runners. Your face is less swollen, I am truly sorry. You're looking lovely, that's if you don't mind an old man telling you?"

"That's okay, Shaun."

"It's the bikers, my mates. The Harrier's, especially the Hen's. They like to sit around and chat and only pay when they leave. Even then, they may go off for a spin and come back for a few more hours, before picking up the tab. We don't take the money up front, we take it just before they leave; like they do abroad. That's why my dad called this café The Continental." She stifled her laugh, as she realised he was serious.

"I owe you so much already. You just don't realise how your money saved me for a start."

"Guilt money."

"No, thoughtful; and you were kind and loving and a great shag yesterday."

"I think you mean today!" Shaun corrected her with a mock yawn.

"Oh! Gosh! Yes… really; you were most urgent, and I was far from disappointed."

"I think I surprised myself, it's been such a long time. Listen, pet," he said. "I can see that you are in some kind of shit, you seem really stressed. Especially yesterday. You're looking more relaxed and even lovelier today. It's not a chat up line, honest, although I do fancy you, if truth be known."

"I don't mind. I like being chatted up, especially by someone I have already slept with." He laughed; she smiled. Thoughts of *riding out* clearly in her mind.

"I was never one for the chat. It's been a long time."

"You're not doing too badly."

"I want to know what's going on with you. Are you trying to avoid someone? Why didn't you want to phone the police from here and report 'the yobs' attempted rape yesterday? And Dorset Square, that's top money. What's that all about. Are you a sex worker?"

"Good God! No, nothing like that."

"Well, sorry, but, what's with your *'je suis Zaks chienne'* tattoo? Are you married? Is he after you? I just want to know who's scaring you and how I can help? You can tell me if you're an illegal immigrant or escaped sex worker or both. I'm not a snitch, but if it's none of my business, just say."

She made up a story, not exactly off the cuff, because she had given some thought to the contents of the tale she might divulge and which she may not. She told him there were powerful people who thought she was dead as they had tried to kill her, in a fume filled car, and she believed they think that they have succeeded. So she was trying to keep a low profile, while she tried to investigate her detractors. She told him she had specific information they want to suppress and would suppress by all and every means, and that included murder. Then she told him about the Picasso photographs of Gertrude and Alice B Tochlas and her Courtauld Institute studies and dissertation and how she had the key to their compromising pornographic photographs, and how their publication would devalue all the Picasso's in private hands and museums and people would lose loads of dollars as his reputation would be devalued, big time, and... he interrupted before she could finish.

"Now. You tell me the real reason you are agitated and trying to keep a low profile from someone, something, including the law, young lady," he said decisively. "That was nonsense, and you know it. Piccaso's reputation would be enhanced."

As soon as she caught his cold disproving gaze, her eyes prickled and her throat tightened. The sudden feeling of being alone again left her speechless. She was overwrought, as he could clearly see, and she was desperate to tell him everything; but she knew that to do so would be stupid. He helped her up and took her through to his room, asking his assistant for two more fresh coffees and later he brought them through.

Rebecca knew she was going to tell Shaun the moment he put a comforting arm around her waist, she just capitulated and unburdened her anxieties and told him: not about Q and not about the scam, but about the fume filled car in the tunnel, the attempted murder, the Indian clinic, her love for Lochy, the father of her baby, and how she felt so guilty about sleeping with him, Shaun (although she lied, because she didn't.) About Dianne, now Mrs Majewska, and the sham marriage that had probably embezzled her rightful inheritance from her uncle, her ex-guardian, because both her parents were killed in a plane crash when she was only 14, and how they only found her mum's ring, and how she wanted to kill Dianne or Lochy or both of them... And this time he did believe her.

***

He believed her, not just because she appeared desperate, but also because her obvious trauma exposed the truth in her eyes; a dark pool of depth, welling up in a plea for his help. As he considered her dilemma, he felt an overwhelming desire to tell her his story. As he felt so much guilt, a guilt time had blurred, but not suppressed. She knew he had been in prison, but not the circumstances that led to his incarceration. Circumstances, Shaun had tried to bury under the constant rigmarole of the day-to-day management of his café, with the anger release of competition rugby and a strict fitness regime.

He told her he had killed his own wife, Mavis. Pleaded guilty and done his stretch, but, he assured her, his wife's death was not premeditated in any way, because he loved her whole being, through and through, with all his heart and he missed her every day, even now, seven years later. Every single day.

He had confessed, of course, he said, and went down for second degree murder.

He had broken her neck, in a jealous rage when he found her fucking with his mate. Found them at it. If he had found out later, he said he would have been devastated, although, he would have acted differently, most definitely acted differently. Non-violently. He had gone over and over the moment a thousand times and he can still hear her neck snap: every time, he said. It seems that he didn't think of hitting his mate.

Everything to do with his trial, the media interest; the whole situation, killed off his mum, he believed, while he was inside prison and his dad gave up his own life, a year after Shaun's release. He was allowed out of prison, for an afternoon, just for his mum's funeral, and seeing his old dad and some of the café clientele again, gave him the impetuous to stay clean and get early parole.

"I had five years of anger management at her majesty's pleasure and I still lashed out at you. I'm sorry."

"Memory reflex, I think I read somewhere, Shaun, unless, like the Nike Sports Adverts suggest, you think more of your trainers than you do of your girl?" he laughed. And it lightened their mood.

Rebecca felt much better within herself, and calmer. More rested mentally than she had for days. The feeling that Shaun was with her, on her side, caring about her and for her, was reassuring.

Shaun seemed to believe she was in real, if not mortal danger, and agreed to undertake some research for her the following day as one of the *Harrier's* was a police officer, a motor cycle cop, who could probably find information on Lochlan's VW Polo. They agreed to meet the following afternoon and she thanked him on leaving and kissed him lightly on the lips at the door. How lovely to have to stretch up and kiss someone on my tippy toes, she thought.

***

Lochlan had asked for a meeting with the head of the security personnel who inhabited the mews house at the end of the PM's garden. As the PM was still not in residence, there was only one or maybe two security operatives, possibly just looking at screens he surmised. He had been told he must not leave the building *of his own accord* until Rebecca Stein was found as he was her lure and, *they feared for his well-being.* This obscure phrase meant he was still on sabbatical leave from UCL and although he had appeared on television chat shows, he was taken and returned in Dianne's old Volvo to avoid any unhealthy interest in his celebrity. She had to drive and accompany him teasing him mercilessly about his TV make up as he removed it in transit. He knew that she was only getting at him, because she thought he was a wimp. Although, he was aware that he wasn't good company as he was maudlin and thoroughly fed up. He would have been deflated anyway, after the euphoria that accompanied these appearances, as he felt a double whammy due to his actual lack of freedom. Always re-emphasised when he had to be 'smuggled' in and out of TV Studios.

***

Dianne had separate accommodation across the whole of the attic (that included Lochlan's house and the PM's) with views from the dormer windows over the private park garden at the front and views over the rear garden to the Mews houses, including the ally and the refuge bins. The cook and cleaner, a man and wife team, lived in the basement. They had trouble with foxes tackling the old refuge bins, so now the bins had locking handles and a light had been installed in the alley approach as a further deterrent. In the past, when alerted by noises in the back alley, Dianne would move onto her attic terrace, the telescopic night sights of her cross bow focused, the bolt in tension, ready and waiting. She had shot several foxes over the years.

Dianne had lived in the same attic apartment for a decade, since her mid-twenties. One room was a private gym containing her purpose-built fitness equipment. She had shared the gym with the previous incumbent of the house who had a Fatwa bestowed upon him, now lifted, or so she was led to believe. She had a whole shelf of trophies from body building competitions including a Miss Universe in which she obtained a bronze medal, (and as she constantly topped up her suntan on her tiny terrace or in the conservatory) Lochlan told her, that bronze was probably deserved. On the second shelf was her target shooting medal, for a third at the National Championships, Bisley. An achievement for which she was rightly proud. However; on the top shelf was her pride and joy, the crystal glass trophy she had won the previous year for being the fastest female in the Wanaka Triathlon, (held annually in New Zealand) while beating most of the men. She was training to defend her title, jogging frequently around the private garden early mornings, in the hope that the real Mrs Majewska would turn up soon, dead or alive, in time.

If Lochlan wanted to go for a walk around the private park garden on his own, security agreed, because Dianne could see him from her windows and unknown to him, he was also tagged.

Any exit from the park would have alerted her bleeper and she was also able to hear any conversations he may have with the park staff or others via the same equipment.

**

Lochlan could frequently be seen just walking and sometimes heard, talking to himself. Worrying signs. After all, security were only looking after his welfare. They had told him that there were factions who had threatened to decapitate him or worse; what could possibly be worse, he wondered. Security did not explain further. There was also a lot of fan mail, from women mainly, who wanted to marry him and have his babies, not even singular, and not always single; some wanted to mother him. True there were some men who called him 'a diva'. Time to ditch the pink duvet, he thought. He had never known anything like it. He realised Q had made headlines internationally and he had been subsequently elevated to a *Mature Celebrity* status, but he still felt he hadn't done anything extraordinary and he certainly didn't feel mature. He had been on TV, (especially when the News of Q was first brokered) and beamed through the eyes, ears and brains of at least 2 billion people. So what, he thought. It doesn't mean a thing, people even want to marry serial killers on death row. And he felt like he was on death row. Fame, 'Jesus', he thought. I would settle for fifteen minutes now and be done. Hindsight. Bugger hindsight. What's the use of being able to afford a top of the range auto, when you are forced to be driven around in an old Volvo so that people don't recognise you. His mother had often told him that fame and fortune was a hollow crown, as did JC's sayings on the Q tablets and old Bill Shakespeare as well of course. "Hindsight; fucking hindsight," Lochlan said out loud, before resuming his contemplation. Rebecca had mentioned that Ted Turner and Jane Fonda often ate together in a two-bit Italian restaurant in down town New York, (to canoodle and chat incognito) although people recognised them, they were never challenged as the locals thought. *No! Can't be them, with all their money they would eat up town.* Madness, enough money between them to buy Manhattan, and they eat in the equivalent of The Continental and drive there in a tin pot car. He wanted out, he wanted to walk across Victoria park to The

146

Dolphin pub and down a pint, on his own, in his own time and quite honestly, get totally pissed and fall over. "Where the fuck are you Becky," he said out loud.

***

Shaun had set to his task like a man on a mission. He believed of course that Rebecca was in imminent danger (as indeed she was) and so he used his network of bikers to answer some of her questions. His traffic police contact, Terry, had confirmed that Lochlan's VW Polo was registered to a Professor Lochlan Majewski of number 12 b Park View, Hackney, but as the previous owner; the new owner was a Mrs Rebecca Vera Majewska, his wife, living at the same address. There were reverberations and murmuring among the Hackney Harriers as their long-time member and some would say buddy, Matthew Reynolds, was exposed as an undercover cop: well there wasn't proof, but his name came up against the VW (Marco) Polo search, (after it was found in The Hamlets archway and impounded by the police) and Terry had noticed a code number which alerted other serving officers to an officer who was working under cover.

Shaun had also been industrious and built up a comprehensive profile on Dianne. Dianne Mayhew-Robinson. Only child of General Sir Mayhew-Robinson. Brought up on hunting with hounds, and equestrian pursuits. Grouse and pheasant shoots, fly fishing, rowing, fencing, tennis, lacrosse. She was highly competitive, yet always saying please and thank you and showing magnanimity to the losers. Superb athlete, superb shot, great horsewoman, triathlon supremo and fully trained in armed or unarmed combat once she had been recruited by our secret services when still an 'A' level student at Cheltenham Ladies College. Her father was delighted, (although he was not supposed to know.) Partly because she was his heir and only child and partly, because she and he thought that she was his son.

Dianne was only 18 and stubbornly refusing to further her education in any field at University as she was in the planning stages of circumnavigating the globe by cycling, swimming and canoeing. She still hoped the journey might be possible, once her *old man had popped his clogs* as she once put it. Not that he or she comprehended the working-class origins of the phrase. 'The

Service' had a very high opinion of her professionalism which had been proven in her guardianship of persons who necessitated a safe house. Her sexual preferences were well known to MI6 (but not to her parents) as she already frequented the exclusive Dugout Club near Cirencester, (housed underground in a defunct nuclear bunker,) when recruited.

Her interests were also explicitly understood by the Hackney Harriers, as she was an honorary member of the Barbie faction. Women who had their own motorbikes or rode pillion, drank pints and liked a bit of rough. All of them had a variety of barbed wire tattoos and piercings on their bodies. There were only a few, but all were tall, and all were blonde, either natural or assisted. They delighted in being known throughout the 'bikers' fraternity as the 'Barbie Dolls'. While all the other women Harriers were known as the 'Hens'.

Little of this information was music to Rebecca's ears, especially the confirmation of Dianne's sham marriage to Lochlan and his own, apparently willing presence at the ceremony. What was most disconcerting to Rebecca: the flat-share in Marylebone was found to be registered in her own name and not Rosey's and even her uncle was a signing witness to the agreement. This information finally galvanised her actions, as she knew she had to ask Shaun to stop all enquiries as the consequences could be too dangerous for him and her. His biker pals were also worried that there might be another 'Mat the Rat', (as they now referred to the deceased police informer) in their midst as not all Hells Angels are angels that is. She told Shaun to ease off for his own safety.

"Why? Rebecca. Why? For fucks sake," Shaun asked. "What can you possibly know that's that big, that dangerous?"

"I can't tell you, not anything, it's much too dangerous," she emphasised.

"Come off it, Becky, you're having me on. Really? Like what for Christ's sake, like what?"

"Let's just say it could be much like being in possession of the irrefutable proof that none of the West's nuclear capability was in fact capable or fit for purpose."

"That big, really? That's nonsense, isn't it? That's got to be bullshit. That big? Is that it?"

"If it wasn't bullshit."

"Really Beck, it can't be that big as you wouldn't stand a chance of surviving if you have proof of something similar that's that big. There were guys in Strangeways Prison who would lie you on a work bench and squeeze your bollocks in a vice until you told them where your 'snout' was stashed, let alone a state secret."

"No! Not at all like that, that is not it, no, but what I do know for sure is even bigger than that speculation, much bigger, honest, but the proof has been lost. You must believe me Shaun, and don't look at me like that, it's truly huge, please stop, for me, you must, please. You've been most helpful, really, but it is dangerous to continue, I promise you. I like you too much to risk losing another friend."

Although convinced Rebecca faced an imminent death threat, Shaun still thought a criminal gang or hit-man may be the cause of her distress, (related in some way to her 'je suis Zak's chienne' tattoo) and not a state secret.

***

Rebecca knew as much as she wanted to know or could know before calling at number 20 and confronting them, Mister and Misses Majewska. Now she was more than scared as she clearly understood that she may be going to her death and the death of her child. She really did not know what to expect. She was nervous, in case, behind their closed door there could be representatives from The Brethren just waiting. That impending motherhood had been the main precursor of her strength and determination and not just her feelings for Lochy, she now realised. Partly due to Shaun's presence, but, also because she was doubting Lochy's sincerity. She had given a lot more thought to parenting since her last scan; his last scan, the grainy grey shadow of his pulsating heart. The excitement and miracle of giving birth. Yet she was terrified of the potential responsibility of another human relying on her for its every need. She had concentrated so much on her and her child's survival and at times, (most of the time she realised) she was in denial. Almost as if she was playing a part, a role, like uncle Paul. The miracle seemed more real the closer that she came to the inevitability of giving birth.

Rebecca longed for her previous life. It had only been a few weeks since her visit to Lord Soane's Museum with her dear uncle, but it seemed an age and it had aged her. Almost four months ago she was a carefree student of Art History at Berkeley University, studying a subject of choice, not of necessity, and not for any foreseeable employment. She had studied compulsively, recognising that her ability to undertake her studies was entirely due to her parents' premature death, and the legacy she received. She clearly felt that she owed them. She was so pleased to be taking part in a 'real life' after all her previous setbacks, and addictions. Two years of regular therapy, (in Berkeley, California) with the same consultant, had apparently, restored her confidence and reformed her more outgoing, creative personality. Moving on to a post grad in London, eventually, after undertaking a client project for her uncle. Feeling up beat on meeting with friends. Visiting museums, cinemas, theatres, shopping, reinforcing her belief in herself. She had also embraced the flat-share with Rosemary Gibbs, (a developing close friendship) while soaking up the delights of the City of London. Now, however, her all-consuming anxieties had returned, understandably, as she was a mother-to-be with an indeterminate future, which might be terminated, sometime soon.

She knew she should have called into number 20 earlier; but it was the possibility that it was Lochy's car, his VW Marco at both crime scenes. His marriage; to *her,* Dianne, Rebecca's nemesis. Above all, his dubious integrity. His conviction volte-face. This had troubled and stopped her. This impossible charlatan, Professor Lochlan Majewski, was the man she was determined to see tomorrow. The father of the child she carried, whom, she thought, may have been so naïve, or willingly corrupted, to put his name to the second biggest religious deception in history. Unless of course, she considered, (offering up a quiet prayer) Jesus was the son of God.

***

Rebecca and Shaun were not allowed to park the car in the street in front of the terrace as a man approached them, asked them their business and showed them where to park. She informed Shaun, this amount of security probably meant the PM was at home. She assumed the number plate of Shaun's Fiat would have been noted by security, researched, and the information perused before he had turned off the engine. Even his and her face may have been recorded and matched against a database of several thousand images. However, it was more likely that they were expected, as security moves in mysterious ways and can wait unobtrusively until more certain of a conviction. Shaun said, he would go with her for support, and she was pleased, as her nerves were rippling. Still, '*age quod agis*'. She knew it had to be. However, he wasn't at all happy when she asked him to wait in the car.

She made slow, but purposeful strides towards No 20, walked up the steps to the front door of the Majewska's house with a thumping heart and a weakening resolve, taking deep breaths, steadying herself on the hand rail. The over-glossed black door towered above, polished brass door-handles and letter boxes winked back at her. She stood on the top step in turmoil, glancing back at the car. Shaun gave a double thumbs up encouragement.

During the past four days while Shaun researched into the various facets of Rebecca's case, she had worked at the Orchid and then rested in her little room. She had made the most of her looks as one of the Thai girls had cut and styled her hair, but in truth, even in adversity she was truly beautiful. After trying on several garments, belonging to Nombel, (the only house mate close to her size, although not so tall) she settled on a black dress with a high neck and a few sparse, but colourful embroidered flowers running diagonally from her left shoulder to right hip. She wore her own linen jacket, chosen by her mysterious dresser. The thought still wrangled her.

Still hesitating on the top step, Rebecca didn't feel ready, but she was ready. There was no bell, so she lifted and let drop the heavy knocker. In the shortest time that can seem an age: the door was opened by the housekeeper. She gave her name and was asked to wait in the vestibule, while the housekeeper, walked up the wide and elegant staircase to inform Professor Lochlan that she was here. After hanging up her jacket and a new sling bag in the large hallway, she waited nervously at the bottom of the stairs, half expecting to be intercepted, frisked and handcuffed by security guard's. Suddenly she heard Lochlan's voice cry out.

"Becky, Becky, Oh! Becky," as he ran down the stairs towards her, his face beamed with delight. Tripping up near the bottom, he parted company with his flip flops, and exhibiting a forward dive worthy of their name, he hit the beautiful polished terrazzo floor. It was only the front door that stopped him. He no longer looked happy.

"Lochy my love, my love, my love," Rebecca said as she attempted to roll him over.

"Don't move him," the naked Dianne ordered as she called down from the top of the stairwell.

"Saw it all on the monitor," she said, as she continued jangling down the stairs. "Thank God you're here."

Dianne was checking Lochlan all over for damage, looking into his eyes and ears before slowly and carefully turning him onto his side with Rebecca's concerned help. Dianne's naked breasts and bottom, well, *a woman's wobbly bits* as the bin man said, in all positions. She even noticed Dianne had several more barbed wire tattoos on her body. It was the barbed wire tattoo lines around her nipples that unnerved her. Glimpses of her labia lips, including the five rings, she could deal with. What the devil was she doing upstairs naked with my Lochy? Was her first thought, as she watched her rapid athletic decent.

"No broken collar bone, ribs... not fractured, he's breathing. Okay, he'll live. I pressed the emergency button for doctor Sif, as I saw Lochlan fall, he will be here soon. Just a minute, he's puckering up."

"Oh Becky, there you are," Lochlan said, "I have missed you. They, she; (he looked disapprovingly at the naked Dianne) have taken over my life."

***

Shaun sat for some time listening to a sports commentary, but as he had had no communication from Rebecca, he drove back to his Café. He didn't realise of course, at the two houses, all mobile phone communication would be blocked when the PM is 'in house' as cell phones can be used to trigger explosives or incendiary devices. She didn't realise that herself until later, and rushed outside to tell him, but he was gone, although she did phone him at the Continental on the land-line to thank him and to let him know she was staying the night, as she was waiting for Lochlan to come home from the clinic where doctor Sif had sent him for x-rays. A private clinic, she was unimpressed. No waiting around in A&E for the Professor, she thought, although he did have to wait ages for his ambulance. "Somnambulance that was," he said when the ambulance finally arrived. *Boom-Boom.*

Rebecca no longer found his humour funny. She wanted to confront him alone and when he was more recovered. This was certainly not the time. She was genuinely pleased by his evident delight on seeing her and she had faltered, but she was committed to get to all the facts from Lochlan and Dianne about the situation. Therefore, she decided to take up Dianne's offer and ask Dianne if she may stay the night, as she had invited her up to her 'Pad' for a coffee. Dianne had said she had been given the okay to answer any of Rebecca's questions, truthfully; if she was able. She seemed quite forthright and straightforward, and Rebecca was beginning to like her. Which was not her plan, in fact Lochlan's accident had put the skids under her intended vehemence, which was rightly heart felt and more than justified. Such as:

Why the fuck did you get married to that naked, robotic, androgynous, tattooed tart in the first place? And what's more; why didn't you ask me? WHACK!!!

***

Dianne's apartment was clean, minimal, functional and tasteful. The kitchen was part of a spacious interior that went right across the two houses. No. 20 and 21. Rebecca didn't comment as she knew 21 was the PM's house. Uncles revelation that *a prominent politician suggested the scam idea*, crossed her mind. She shuddered at the thought, the connection, the implications.

"This is great coffee Dianne, but I'm not sure it's what I need, I am so wound up."

"It's mid roast Columbian, but it won't wind you up any more. Its decaf."

"Really, that's good."

"You are nervous my girl, I mean, there's no need. You're in a win-win situation. I don't know what developments there have been, or what there for, or why you have been in mortal danger, but I do know you are very lucky to be alive, I mean, your involvement or demise must have been hugely important when you consider what forces have been mobilised on your behalf. I mean, even the head of Homeland Security wishes to see you today."

"Gosh!" Rebecca was stunned. She was still paranoid. *Is she trying to put me at my ease or maybe she doesn't know anything, maybe she is, and has been, following orders. I ought to be careful about what I ask her,* she thought.

"He has told me to answer your questions, I mean, if I can, but he says there are a few questions, only he can answer. We both know our Professor intimately, don't we, I mean, go ahead, just ask."

Rebecca was sat opposite, but close to her, on seating that was placed underneath an enormous dormer window, glazed on the three sides. There was access to a small roof patio with decking. Dianne was still naked.

"Why are you naked, what were you doing up there?"

"Pass…Jesus! I mean, I can't believe that's your first question."

"Oh! Sorry, this is so… you know… so… Why did you move in with Lochy and why did you marry him? For what reason?"

"Well, not because I liked him, that's a given. I was asked to impersonate you and be his wife by my superiors, the best man was your sometime guardian and uncle, the actor Paul Smith. Although I wasn't allowed to mention his stage name to anyone, because he is, sorry, was, quite a celebrity, because the marriage ceremony had to be done on the quiet. Why did you miss his funeral? Everyone who was anyone was there. *Our boys,* were hoping to pick you up."

"Expediency."

"Yes, of course. I guess that I will be in your, I mean, my married role until you and the Professor are resolved. I mean, it's you who are legally married to him. If you don't want to be then it is you that must divorce him, not me. I mean, that way you will gain your half of your uncle's legacy. That's what your uncle Cohen said to me. After his, your uncle's death, I mean, possibly within the year, he said. So, he must have known, you know, heart or something, must have. I am sorry for you, really, but I have no idea. I mean, what it was all about. I just supposed Paul

Smith, your uncle, was also an agent, taking red orders as we all are."

"Dawh! He would have found that hilarious. He couldn't hurt a flea," Rebecca hesitated, suddenly aware of her use of the past tense. A lump in her throat stopped her continuing.

"The marriage was a convoluted method of payment, for a successful outcome, that's all I knew, I mean, all he told me. I think he was, one of ours. Not fully active, more of an AIC, an alternative information channel. Agents, as you must know, have a sentence we can say, to a covert suspect, and if it's answered correctly, we know they are singing off the same hymn sheet, and he answered."

"Correctly?"

"Yes." Rebecca couldn't believe this of her uncle and considered Dianne's comments to be filibustering, just smokes and mirrors to confuse her in her quest. "Quite a few actors are, you know, as they have legitimacy for travel and extended stays abroad, often in hot spots, I mean, as do journalists, authors as well." Rebecca thought all this talk of agents was twaddle. Convinced, her jealousy of the athletic bright-eyed beauty that sat before her, was entirely justified. She cut to the chase.

"I understood the terms of the marriage, but why live with him originally at his apartment if he's not your type?"

"Once again I was asked if I would."

"Or told that you would have to?"

"Yes. Of course. I believe the plan was for me to keep an eye on him, I mean, obviously, and to persuade him to undertake an assignment considered top priority. I mean top. I was asked to ingratiate myself and to report any discrepancies in his personality or life style. Something that may move into the public domain. I am often asked to do this, with both genders, if my superiors hope to recruit someone for something, or promote someone to a higher office, even a prospective Archbishop. To avoid compromises or sometimes, maybe, to compromise, I believe. But we didn't get along, he was lovely, but too nice. I mean, too nice for me anyway. Initially I was informed the assignment may have been for several months, but later I was made to understand, I was just holding someone else's place. After a month they parachuted you in from the states. I guessed your CIA were involved.

That's not a question by the way, I mean, I am under instructions not to ask you any questions, whatsoever."

"Are you really? Poor you. So, you were just keeping my place warm," Rebecca said this with a raised intonation that implied scepticism. "How could he be *too nice,* I have known so many shitty men who could have been *a lot* nicer."

"Oh, come on, you know what I mean."

"I'm surprised. You did have sex, didn't you? He seemed quite needy. I don't mind, well I do mind, but I don't really."

"Sort of, I was just a 'reporter', but he liked taking photographs. I am surprised that you never asked him about me. I mean, I was sure he would have mentioned me. He liked taking photos. But you don't have to worry, I mean, he didn't fancy me, I was unable to tease out any kinks anyway."

Rebecca was thinking, her narcissistic rival probably encouraged Lochy and buggered off with the photographic evidence, for her own perusal.

"He didn't talk about you much, and I didn't want to seem too inquisitive, he didn't even mention your amazing barbed tattoo. It's extraordinary, in a fine blue line. It's very skilfully done?"

"Would you like one?"

"Was that another question?" Rebecca said light-heartedly.

"Oops!"

"Actually, I do understand why Lochy got married to you."

"Oh please, call him Lochlan," Dianne said, "I hate Lochy, it's so domestic."

"Okay. Okay. I know the reason. It was to do with a financial arrangement. I understand; but I just don't understand why he didn't ask me. It's what uncle wanted for us, at the time of his marriage, your marriage, we were getting on fine."

"Well, Rebecca, I understand Lochlan told your uncle that he would prefer a 'paper marriage'. I mean, he insisted. I mean, he seemed certain that you would want a family with all the trimmings. His actual words to me when I questioned him just before the wedding were, something like. *I couldn't marry her Di, she is too needy and it would mean a full commitment to family, and I am committed to my research, I have so many ideas, too much to do, this is my chance, to do something for myself for once, to ditch teaching, to make my way in the world, to stuff all those 'up your ass', complacent academics. Rebecca would want three kids and a budgerigar and follow me around all day.* He was adamant. I mean, your uncle was most disappointed, and left it to the very last minute to change Lochlan's position as he was still trying to persuade, but there was no changing his mind; so eventually I had my orders to go ahead. Any more questions on that one, I mean, that assignment."

"No, I am a bit speechless. Sorry. Just a minute, need to take a breath, must be the coffee," Rebecca hesitated for a few moments to collect her thoughts, while a hundred incidents rapidly searched her memory of the past few months. "Lochlan wouldn't agree to a sham marriage, he's a man of integrity, I am sure, certain: he believes in honesty, truth, and justice." She was beginning to think that maybe Dianne really liked Lochy and was just being bitchy, especially as it now seemed she had not just replaced her, but, 'Jocked-her-off' The Project.

"Well, he believed in marriage even less, I can assure you. I mean, anything else? They will be here soon."

"Yes, yes please. When you moved from Lochlan's place, why did you move in with the undercover cop, Matthew Reynolds?"

Dianne stood up, she flushed, her nipples swelled and there were goose pimples. "Who said he was an UPO? I never knew. Who says? Why do you say that?" Her body rings jangled in annoyance, as she sat down again.

"Was that a question, Dianne?" Rebecca asked quietly, troubled by Dianne's response.

"Yes, if you have an answer. No if you don't."

"I don't have anything definite." She was surprised by Dianne's reaction to Matthew's name, acting as though she more than liked him, or something. "I know, I'll tell you everything I know if you do likewise. What do you think?"

"I think it sounds like a game we used to play in the dorm," Dianne said with irritation.

"Oh, my God yes, so it does, okay, we will play that as well, later." And they both did laugh. A laugh of mutually understood vulnerability. Both having been used by men in some way, always.

"All I know, everything I know, is that Matthew was working for us and was instrumental in taking you away from Lochy, sorry, Lochlan, to make room for me."

"That's it? I mean, I knew that. I only saw him weekends anyway."

"Yes, that's all I know."

"You said that he was a UPO, if he was, I am severely compromised."

"Yes, we believe he was."

"That's it then. So, it wasn't an accident."

"Is that a question?"

"No, a statement."

"You were fond of him?"

"No, Rebecca, I loved him." Dianne seemed all dithery, trying desperately to be professional and composed. "That's my career on hold then. Look, I need to dress as your people have arrived. I mean, don't look so surprised, I do wear clothes. I just love to be without, feeling at one with oneself, when around the house, don't you? And naked in front of people you know intimately, no problem. I don't come down naked, as a rule. This morning was an exception, I had to move quickly, I mean, it could have been the spine. I have been around horses, fallen riders. Then it seemed silly to go and change. I realise it was awkward for you. Also, for me."

"Yes, well, the doctor wouldn't notice either I guess."

"Good God. No, he's my doctor, not the Prof's. Why don't you sit out on the terrace and I will bring you another drink, you will be meeting your people soon and you will have to talk to Gerald out there as he chain-smokes."

Rebecca opened the sliding doors to the terrace decking. It was a long way down and she could see across a vast area of London. She was pensive, the confused brain needing a rest from incomprehension. The overview of Paris from Sacre-Coeur, seemed to contain dark grey and white, like fish pie, she thought, but this view is more rust-ochre-cream, like the English apple pie and custard uncle Paul used to love. She was immediately upset by her thoughts of her Uncle and withdrew from the balustrade and the inviting drop to oblivion. Then she noticed the refuge bins, she squirmed. What stupidity, she thought. Dianne must have seen me, and security must have been aware, just waiting for me to mess up I guess, unless they were just testing me, pushing me to my limit, to make me do something stupid, or suffocate even. Maybe they were hoping that I would enter the private areas, where I could legitimately be arrested. Or, maybe, she considered, the PM was not in the building and I just got lucky. Although security wouldn't be disturbed by any noise, as at that time of night, security would be expecting the rumpus of the trash men.

Dianne came back wearing a smart light blue twin set, with navy blue fine denier tights and court shoes, quite 'County', Lochy would have called her, she thought. She had pulled herself together and looked calm, setting a tray down with a range of herbal teas and a flask of hot water.

"It's for the guests, so do help yourself."

"Tell me again, who are the guests?"

"Your people. I mean, the head of Homeland Security, who is the PM, and the chief of our Secret Service. Bernard Thorpe, Lord Thorpe."

"In what regard Dianne?

"In what regard? In what regard? … Golly you're a cool one. Surely you know? They put a Red alert out on you several weeks ago, from the top, I mean, from the very top mind you. You were so hot you were smoking. We heard through The Network that Red was now Blue. The guy that got you out of your near fatal situation, will probably get a citation. I mean, I do admire your ability to go underground. Did you stay in London? You were not picked out on any CCTV footage and they had the usual teams working overtime, and the big boys have image enhancers. You must be one of their best."

"No, I am not anything really, I have been in London, and mainly Hackney and here, I smashed my face, banged it badly, in a car accident. I'm caked in make-up now as you can see. I guess the CCTV couldn't photo fit, maybe, but I have been staying at a Thai restaurant and spent some time in a clinic. In recovery."

"Yes, I noticed that you had taken a hit; although I wasn't allowed to ask how. That's probably it. I guess it must have been much worse originally. At which clinic and restaurant did you say?"

"Well now, yes, the one down the road, actually I didn't say. I'm not allowed to." Suddenly thinking it was probably not a good idea to give details as she remembered the gun downstairs in her new sling bag, and James, the Orchids owner, had been good to her, and Mel was connected, and Dianne obviously wants to know what CIA mission was so big. Rebecca changed tack. "It's been a struggle at times as the international assignment had huge implications."

"I bet. I never get any of the exciting stuff, although I am combat ready. I mean, Lochlan's dive down the stairs has been the most exciting thing that's happened here for ages, although you wouldn't want to give him the kiss of life. Oops sorry, of course you would."

"I can see your life here could be dull. I never found life with him dull, far from it."

"I never said he was dull, no way, he's full of surprises. I mean, it's just that he is an irascible academic, I mean, do not play chess with him if you want an early night, he takes an age over every move; or cards as he cheats: or argue, I mean, you cannot win an argument as he thinks he is always right and goes on and on, until you give in."

"Yes, that's true, but then he often is, you know, right. But he wouldn't cheat, not Lochy, sorry."

"I know. I mean, no he wouldn't, not for anything serious perhaps, but he is a rogue, a loveable one at times, but none the less, I can't wait to get rid of him. I mean, it's just that he's been getting on my nerves, slopping around the house feeling sorry for himself; sulking over his loss of you and bursting into tears at the slightest provocation. I mean, he really blubbers. He's quite emotional, isn't he? And he does cheat, he's been gambling big time, almost every day. And half the night, he settles down to study his racing form books as if he was researching a specialist subject in the British Library. I think he is 'losing it' Rebecca, I mean, he even puts bets on three or more horses to win, in the same race and if one *comes in*, as he puts it, he says he has *the* winner. I mean, he never mentions the others, although he bounces around the room like... Oh dear, the blue light's on, that means we have just a few minutes before they come through. I have to turn the heating up and open a bottle, red usually, to let it breathe. I will bring you a glass. I mean, do have some with them."

Rebecca instinctively tapped her tummy, but instantly withdrew her hand and stifled an impending comment. Dianne shot her a telling glance and left.

***

Lochlan was on his way home with slight concussion, two bruised ribs on his left side and a broken big toe were left to heal via rest only. His scraped left hand was bandaged, and the fractured wrist encased in plaster. He had enjoyed the nurse's attention and he was so relieved to have Rebecca back. He was beside himself with indignation for ruining the reunion. Normally if anyone had said they were 'beside themselves with indignation' he would say, *and what was she doing there? Boom-Boom.* As for Rebecca, the fizz had gone out of his boom as far as she was concerned, he realised. Because of the fractures, bruising, and the bump on his head he was confined to bed.

***

Lord Thorpe and the PM arrived through the adjoining door between the two properties, although it was only the attic apartments that interconnected. Dianne introduced them and the PM asked for a normal Café latte and Rebecca joined him. Lord Thorpe sat outside on the terrace. The PM sat where Dianne had been seated as she had gone to her fitness room.

"First of all, I would like to thank you, young lady for your invaluable work on Q and of course you will be 'My Lady' soon, as I have included Professor Majewski in my final honours list." She just couldn't register what was being said, (an honour that made Lochlan a Knight of the Realm, a 'Sir', and part of the establishment) and she went to thank him intuitively, (as he was all smiles) and she was nervous, but stopped when she remembered she was in the presence of a man she despised as he had manifestly contributed to everything she endured during the past four months, wondering what process they may be considering to silence her.

"He won't accept, I know it." Her observation was ignored.

"Now Bernard," the PM pointed to the terrace, "has no idea what The Project was or what Q was all about."

"You mean he thought it was all a brouhaha and he wasn't aware of the huge sham, the scam, your big damn lie?"

"Well, I wouldn't use those terms if I were you, Mrs Majewska, but the services of which he is the CO are unaware that the reason I am talking to you is Q. We were forced to use our secret services to locate you, but intervene to avoid your capture and interrogation, by Bernard's lot, once your uncle's misappropriation threw us off plan. So; when he talks to you later, you may not mention anything to do with Q. And that includes me, of course. Only eight people know about Q's true origins, including yourself and Professor Majewski."

"Professor Lochlan doesn't know anything; nothing at all. I'm sure he never suspected you and your cronies' grand deceit. That's why he came across to the media convinced of Q's authenticity."

"He does now. I have just told him everything," she recoiled. Feeling a wash of heat or energy shimmer through her whole body.

"Lochlan knows! Oh my God! He knows? Poor Lochy. Oh dear! Jesus! Everything?"

"Yes: including your part in this whole business I'm afraid. We…well… I, thought it was only fair to bring him on board, so he would temper his rhetoric and stop him from relating his glib explanations of The Miracles to the media and undermine their mystery and therefore Q. He was quite troubled I believe and persisted in protesting his innocence, although I suspect he may have known all along, don't you?"

She was stunned into a moist eyed silence, and a bemused PM waited for Rebecca to compose herself.

"Temper his rhetoric! Temper his rhetoric! Oh dear… What about my uncle, my guardian, my friend and also Rosey, Rosemary Gibb's?"

"Well. Your uncle committed suicide by deliberate over exertion as I understand it. Bernard will fill in the details for you; but my main reason for talking to you, and I'm afraid, it has to be swift, because I have another appointment. But my main reason, is that your uncle thought a great deal about your well-being. Peter Mackenzie, his legal secretary, and partner I believe, a very accomplished commercial solicitor and estate lawyer, it would seem by all accounts, drew up his will, the actor Paul Smith, aka Simon Cohen's, last will and testament and laid the irrefutable foundations for your survival."

"Really, *my survival*? My word you are a callous man. How come, by what means? May I see it?"

"Yes of course, Bernard has the exact details. It clearly stated that you must be married to Majewski, Professor Majewski, before the shares allocated to The Project, for the Professor and your services, could be transferred. Bernard will fill in the details. But also, your disingenuous uncle, had possession of Lord Soane's tablets.

"He had them? No way, ha, ha, really? So, he had them?" *'Hard core in the caretaker's car park'* the deceptive old bugger, she thought.

"Yes, all of them. That he presumably had stolen, or acquired, from the ICE, the very tablets that contained Q."

"Allegedly."

"All right! All right. Allegedly: deposited in a vault, your family vault. This has forced our hand. Bernard will fill in the legal details, but in consequence, the contents of the tablets were to become common knowledge on your death at any time in the next 60 years if your demise was believed to be suspect. i.e. not definitively by natural causes. *Inappropriate circumstances...* I believe that's the wording, Bernard..."

"...Will fill in the details," Rebecca said interrupting. "You must mean the lack of content relating to Q. N'est ce pas?"

"Yes."

"Fucking hell, ooh! clever old uncle Paul."

"Rather too clever for our liking, young lady, although it's all credit to his legal secretary Mackenzie, he produced a full proof document that stitched us up every which way. Unfortunately, we can't risk asking our legal team to find loop holes without compromising our position."

"Your position."

"Your position as well Mrs Majewska. Now I must go, but it has been a pleasure to meet you and congratulations also on eluding Bernard and his team for so long. You are a remarkable young lady, with a capital L now."

The PM then shook her hand and walked her through to the terrace telling Bernard, that she was all yours and he would meet him tomorrow evening at their weekly briefing.

Rebecca was just thrilled to think her dear uncle had put so much in place for her, and of course, he knew she wanted Lochlan's baby, hence the marriage stipulation, although Lochy would have had to be married to me or my passport, she ventured, to get any money. Maybe that was the plan from the inception. No wonder they asked Dianne, safer all round, she is obviously secure, but doesn't know anything about Q it would seem. It was more likely *they* were going to do the financial transaction that way anyway, uncle would have included the caveat when he realised my feelings for Lochy and our child. It wasn't just luck that there were two Rabbi Simon Cohens registered, with one an American, when Lochy checked. All this forward planning. Maybe Lochy knew Q had to be a scam from the beginning, from the very beginning, in the grand plan. Although he's palpably irreligious, he still seemed convinced that we were privileged to be working on such valuable and ancient texts.

He, Lochy, also believed, (as she had often told him) she loved him. Which did scare him it would seem, as he was always unnerved by her declaration and he was never reciprocal. I did love him, and I still do, she told herself, after all he appears to be the innocent amongst all these self-important conmen. Poor Lochy, she thought. Even Dianne obviously doesn't like him, and he spends so much time with her. What did she call him? An 'irascible academic and a cheat'. I guess he could be, men have always hoodwinked me, always; including uncle Paul, if he was an unlikely paid informer. They both managed to keep the marriage a secret from me. So; he may have known.

***

Lord Thorpe, Bernard Thorpe. Head of The UK Secret Services sat at the terrace table in full sun, opened a silver attaché case, took out his cigarettes, offered one to Rebecca, she declined, and lit his own. He was tall and thin, but expensively dressed and well presented. He was in his mid-fifties, with a full head of silver grey hair, although his clothes, the collar especially, looked one size too big. His shirt and tie were the same mid grey as his suit and silk socks that slipped into black patent leather hand-made shoes. He had cold, pale blue unblinking eyes, almost opal, and a false thin mouthed smile. Then he slowly and methodically, unwound the sunshade, and sat down again.

She had been instantly afraid of him, although he was able to put Rebecca at her ease when he said that he had worked with her father in The Yemen and was particularly complementary about her father's character and he seemed genuinely moved by his untimely death. She went to ask a question, but Lord Thorpe switched into professional mode.

"The best way to handle this, my dear, is for me to tell you everything I know; that is, *we* know. It is best if you do not interrupt, my dear. You will get it all just once. Any questions at the end." She hated being referred to as *my dear.*

"You are a Jew as was Cohen and we believe the assignment must have been one of Mossad's. We have never been told what your 'assignment' entailed, but it was obviously top draw and we know it was concluded successfully, so well done my dear." He took a plastic bag from his case and handed it to her. "This is your uncle's mobile phone and note book retrieved from Bethnal Green Police. The letter taken from your Dorset Square flat is included advising you to collect, it is just routine. We realised you had been back to your shared flat, so you would have seen Miss Gibbs body, that was a mistake. We are extremely sorry. You entered when our boys were in the process of *hoovering* the place. Lucky for you, my dear, that they were able to hide on the balcony. Our boys were under instructions to eliminate the tenant at 19 a. ASAP, promoting suicide. The evidence being only photographic of course. They informed HQ that they had been successful." She gasped at this news. "Shortly after you left, they took your prints and some DNA samples, just routine, although you were on the police data bank however, flagging up your visit."

"Dear me, dear me, no, no, I as good as killed her. I can't live with that, I just can't. Her poor family."

"It's okay, my dear, her death was recorded as suicide. She was one of ours, Simon Cohen had put you on to her, I think you will find, although someone put her on to Cohen. She was there to keep an eye on you and your associates, to support your covert assignment, I believe. We hadn't realised she was so very loyal to you, apparently; stupidly so, as she certainly knew the score, yet she tried every avenue to discover your whereabouts, waiting in the Park outside the Premier's house, even checking morgues unfortunately, my dear."

"I see, I see, then I did kill her. I killed her. Oh! This is terrible, really. Poor Rosey," she said she loved me. She must have. Oh! What have I done? Questioning herself, and realising

Rosey's murderers were there, in the flat, as she walked naked towards Rosey's body in the bathroom.

"Are you alright, my dear. Shall I continue without interruption?" She nodded as she was too upset to speak.

"Now: Cohen, your uncle, had pancreatic cancer, as you probably knew, my dear," she gasped again, as she didn't know, although she knew he was unwell. Lord Thorpe lit another cigarette and this time she took one, without asking. She had smoked from time to time, but mostly hashish. After the first few drags her head spun and she stubbed it out angrily, overcome by his cold insensitivity and patronising dialogue. "Terminal, he knew he had three to six months, tops. Once he knew you had been abducted, we believe Cohen decided on suicide to set in motion your deliverance and ran to his death, he had angina as well, it would have been quick. The paramedics couldn't resuscitate. He left you a note," he passed her a folder containing a synopsis of her uncle's will and a letter to her, "but no need to read it now, my dear, you have to read between the lines as it's not specific about suicide or his insurances would be null and void. The coroner's verdict was accidental death. His death, and the corresponding will, meant that we had to put out a red alert to cancel your elimination. Too late for Miss Gibbs, I'm afraid, but just in time for you it would seem. After the PM was informed about the contents of Cohen's will and the legal malarkey, he gave finding you top priority. We are not privy to its exact contents, but we know it clearly stipulates that a thorough autopsy by three, yes three, independent forensic experts, should be carried out on your death, to determine cause of death. And the information in your family safe, whatsoever that may be, would be released in any case if you were in any kind of suspicious fatal accident. Of course, when we realised; well, when the PM realised, we had to find you and keep you alive, after our team had recalibrated, even though, maybe, there may have been the chance that you were already eliminated. We have been asked to monitor your good self for your indefinite future, the PM stressed that you should be made aware, my dear."

"Oh really, really. My indefinite future?" Rebecca felt an overwhelming desire to kill this man.

"That's it, Mrs Majewska; The PM says that you can now be reunited with your husband and well, move in below. I'm glad this little interlude is over, and the PM seems well pleased. He has taken his eye off the ball lately and he has been harassing me for updates every hour or so for the past few weeks. You must know something of international importance my dear, and you were also extremely adept at keeping your whereabouts under wraps. Any more questions my dear?"

"Yes, *old boy!* You, pale faced, lanky praying mantis. Who abducted me? I know you know, I do know, you must know; I just remember the telephone kiosk on the corner of the Lincoln Fields, it is then a blank until the Hamlets."

"Sorry, I am not privy to the details. Anything else?"

"Not privy, not privy, fuck you."

"I am not. I assure you, I understand that you were abducted, but I really do not know why or how or what for. We always assumed your assignment was covert, but not one of ours."

"Really, really? What about Matthew Reynolds, a UPO, and his death on the M40?"

"I don't recall the name, sorry."

"Well, fuck you, sir; an undercover police officer. You gotta be privy. You're the head fucking dick, aren't you?" Lord Thorpe was taken aback by Rebecca's vitriol. He also believed she had direct contact with the Mossed or CIA hierarchy and responded.

"Just a sec. My dear, a UPO, of course, why am I not surprised you would know? Miss Stein." Lord Thorpe glanced at his notes. Reynolds…Reynolds. "Ah! Yes, Giuseppe Bianchi. He was someone's 'Ears*',* well, your lots' 'Ears*'*. One of your Mossad boys we assumed as he bypassed our GCHQ."

"Ears?"

"You Americans call them *Snoops.* Listening in, bugs, phone conversations et al, you know, must know, as you didn't register and remained below our radar. He's a mystery, although as he had some dubious connection with Italy's P2, we assumed he was a double agent, after he had hitched up with one of ours. Unfortunately."

Rebecca realised that Dianne couldn't have known.

"Anything else? My dear."

"Yes, can you give me the address of Rosemary Gibb's parents?"

"No, can't do, sorry, policy on agents, a matter of security; as an agent yourself, you must understand, her parents wouldn't know."

"Anything else?" Dumbfounded, she shook her head.

"That's it. I'll be off then."

Lord Thorpe took up his attaché case, stubbed out his last cigarette and after giving her a disparaging glance, he disappeared through the terrace doors. There were four stubbed cigarettes left in the ashtray, her bent unfinished one was still smouldering. After smoothing it straight she finished it, sucking hard. Coughing desperately, she hurriedly poured herself another glass of wine, and just sat there thinking things through. An overwhelming sadness coursed through her, fuelling a clear sense that everything that had occurred during the past few years, since the death of her parents, had happened to someone else. She considered everything. Every situation, good, bad and special. '*Events*' as Lochy would put it: but somehow she was not convinced; they had happened to her at all.

She thought about her Ma and Pa, their death, her loss and her feelings. She had always doted on her dad as he was besotted with her, but the realisation, her mother had loved her so much, she had subdued her maternal instincts, troubled her, as Rebecca came to realise, her own abandonment to boarding schools from an early age was, perhaps, a more traumatic parting than her parents' sudden death.

She also thought about Zak (and the 'cobble cracks' on those streets of Paris, paved with her low life friends) and her rescue from his clutches by her dear uncle. Lovely sweet uncle Paul who held her wrists to stop the bleeding's obvious consequences, and by booking barge holidays that go nowhere, but with imagination can go anywhere two sensual consenting humans may choose. To warm up the turkey, to refrain the insane, to deaden the pain.

She thought about Dianne and her ordered, rational, irrational, double life: taking orders, obeying commands. And liking it. Her leathered love, a commanding UPO, giving orders with relish, sensing the power. And liking it. Individuals licensed to kill; sensing their power. And liking it. Governments and politicians, feeling so important, full of deceit and contradiction, sensing their power. And liking it. The Brethren; abusing and using their power to rewrite history. Lawmakers; moral or municipal, above the laws they make. Enforcers, beyond the laws they enforce. All sensing their power. And liking it.

Rebecca was feeling powerless and other worldly; out of control of the future, her baby, Lochy's baby's future, their future. Especially as Lochlan (the gambler, the mad, silly, irresponsible, irascible, Lochy. The same knowledgeable, educated, bright, witty and well-travelled Professor Lochlan) had proved the dictum, that a high intelligence doesn't discount immense stupidity. Rebecca got up to look over the Terrace balustrade, down to the conservatory below, suddenly she felt like flying.

***

"Hello, Becky, come here, give me a kiss. Ooh! I have missed you. Don't stand there, come here. Look at you with your long legs, and so smart, I love you in a dress." Lochy was confined to his bed, but he still tried to slip his free unbandaged hand up her dress as she kissed him on the cheek, just a peck. She pulled back. He was affronted. Rebecca thought Lochlan was in a sorry state; with his fractured arm in a sling, and with his torso propped up against the pillows in his king-sized bed, he looked diminished. He certainly felt deflated.

"Where have you been? People have looked all over, and I have been worried sick. Why didn't you come and see me earlier? I have been here, in this room, for ages. Just waiting. Forgotten." Professor Lochlan, aka, Sir Lochlan Majewski, had been waiting too long with nothing to do but to contemplate all the situations and sub-defuse that had led to his complete and utterly inexcusable naïvete.

"Je suis desolee, Lochlan, poor you. I have been with the PM and then Lord Thorpe."

"That arse hole Thorpe, he won't see me, and I have even asked through the appropriate channels. What did they want? Told you the truth behind the Soane's Tablets, or lack of truth; did they? Is that why you won't kiss me? They told you I was in on it from inception to deception, did they? And I guess you feel used, cheated, and a bit of a dunderhead? Don't you? You thought that you and your fat fairy uncle had set me up, didn't you? DIDN'T YOU? There is a massive ever fucking expanding universe out there my dear Miss Rebecca Stein, with a trillion

169

suns and a trillion, trillion planets to contemplate and therefore a little manipulation of the fucking facts seems minor in comparison."

"That's like saying *'Pour voir les choses il faut les croire possible'*, it just doesn't stack up Lochy, it just doesn't."

"Is that so, little miss innocent. So, where have you been hiding all this time? Shacked up with your friend Rose, no doubt. We men haven't got a chance, have we? We wine you, dine you and administer to your every need; adore your very being, until we're totally besotted, and then what happens? We're swatted. Well, you're in luck, Becky dear, even my arm has an erection, look." He took his arm from his sling to reveal it encased in plaster. She was not even slightly amused. Rebecca understood Lochlan was one of the eight who knew for certain about the truth behind the lie and she realised that he may well have even fooled the Brethren, if he had always suspected a scam from the beginning. Uncle Paul was sure, she thought, that they had convinced Lochlan, 'Their Project' was kosher, and contemporary references to JC's ministry had genuinely been discovered.

"How long have you known, you little shit. For how long?"

"Come off it, Becky, stop being so damn righteous. Who the hell do you think you are, Mother Theresa? coming onto me in the Orchid saying the crap magician's book was on your reading list. Just as if. Wouldn't surprise me if your uncle left it there. And the next day. There you were walking back and forth past the Continental Café, soon after your 'Uncle Rabbi' had left, and just waiting for me to spot you. I'm not stupid. But it was while we were in the Café and you made reference to *The Project,* that my suspicions were first aroused, although when I checked out your CV, all the other things you said were true, including the Gertrude Stein relationship, amazingly. It was also obvious that they played a recording of Big Ben chimes to fool me as to the whereabouts of The Christian Brotherhood's choice location for my induction. Driving me around and around Kew and Richmond, several times before ending up at the Duke of Northumberland's pile, and not a stone's throw from Kew Green where they picked me up and dropped me off. Who did they think they were fooling?"

"So, you did know! I just can't believe it. Why for fuck sake, Why? You were the person who quoted Battaglia to me. I even wrote it down as I thought it was so beautiful. *I believe in the energy of the earth, the sky, nature, and the energy of love. But most of all I believe in truth, honesty and justice.* That's what you said, JUSTICE," Rebecca shouted the word, "you know Lochy. ACADEMIC RIGOUR. You're the fucking arse hole, not Thorpe. At least he doesn't pretend to be anything else. No wonder you are under house arrest. You're a bastard chameleon, I hate people like you."

"Calm down, my dear," Lochlan said mockingly.

"Don't you fucking well *my dear* me or I will shoot you." Rebecca took out the gun that she had taken from the Orchid's lost property drawer and was pointing it at him. The safety catch was on, but he wasn't to know this. The previously impassioned face of Professor Lochlan Majewski went pastel. He could see she was serious. He also assumed, all Americans knew how to shoot. Mel had often told him Rebecca was in love with him. He was scared. He also knew that he had to talk himself out of this predicament.

"Why? I want to know why?"

"It wasn't for the money or the Knighthood."

"You have accepted Lochy," she interrupted in disbelief, "you have accepted. Don't you know that any person worth their salt would refuse such an honour? Why, even Cliff Richard has one!" She squeezed the trigger menacingly and Lochlan's upper lip shone with sweat.

"Look, *my dear*," he was deliberately being provocative, challenging. "I believed in Q, as you rightly said in French just now *'In order to see things, it is necessary to believe them possible'* I have always believed that Jesus would have provided his sayings and teachings in a written form. If not JC directly, then one or more of his disciples would have done so, in fact, I am sure of it."

"Belief, Lochy, does not justify deceit in my book."

"Well it has in every other religious book that I have studied."

"Boom-Boom, Lochy, *my dear*, you forgot to say, *Boom-Boom*," she said this in a tone that one might use to a child. "And you can't say, *in fact*, Lochy, the point being: there are no facts. Your scam, The Project, presented the Lord Soane's Tablets as facts, just because their proven age, *a fact*, corresponded to JC's period, they have, therefore, been taken as contemporary facts.

But they're not facts, are they Lochy, as the Tablets contained, not a single reference to Jesus or his ministry. Uncle said as much. I just don't know how you can justify the deception, I just don't know. I just thought you were a genuine, honest, sweet guy, and I loved you."

Lochlan thought he was softening Rebecca's resolve. She has called me Lochy several times, he thought. And she had admitted her love for me.

"Look, put the revolver down, sit on the bed and I will explain Becky, I'll explain."

He was wrong. She pulled up a packing case and sat down at the end of the bed, facing him with the gun still clearly aimed between his eyes, she released the safety catch. She knew she had him as she had been through so much, so very much, and surrounded by so much pomposity and deceit, she fully intended to shoot, with little regard for the consequences and at this point he clearly understood he may only have a few minutes to live. He realised that he had to give the oral performance of his life, literally, and talk his way out of this.

"Look Becky, I love you, I love you, truly, don't do it. Listen, you are having a breakdown, you have obviously been having a difficult time. It's not my fault, don't shoot, you're being irrational: put the gun down. Listen, you really need to know or else you will be making a false judgement. Listen, I believed in Q. I truly believed in Q. Just listen to me, give me a hearing at least… Please."

"Okay. I'm listening, but there can be no justification for deceit on any scale and certainly not on such a scale that abuses the historical heart-felt beliefs of millions of Christians world-wide and what's more, has fucked up my life."

"I know, I know, listen. Please give me a hearing, please. At the same time as Christianity, as a philosophy, was gaining a degree of acceptance in the Roman Empire, other realms of thought were in contention. Neoplatonism developing from Plato out of Plotinus' teachings, including a strong anti-materialism, thoughts and ideas from the Far East and Persia, all in a melting pot.

"Stop procrastinating NOW, Lochy. STOP. I'm well pissed off and you're only playing for time," she was shouting again.

Professor Lochlan Majewski, ne, Sir Lochlan Majewski, was in a desperate lecturing mode, a situation at which he was most accomplished, and he was good; mesmeric even. With his penetrating, dark, flashing eyes, he exuded confidence and charm. There was a sing-song rhythm to his delivery and both his phrasing and timing were perfect. It was the reason Professor Summerskill, a rival colleague, referred to him always as, *that stand-up comic.* Rebecca was slowly captivated and drawn in. It was why, as he exuded a passion for a subject, she first fell in love with him.

"This melting pot of ideas, including Judaism, culminated in the first Gospels, and transformed the Roman Empire, but it wasn't destroyed, it was only subsumed. 'Seguir la corriente' was the motto of the period. We still have The Holy Roman Empire coming to a church near you, throughout the world, even today."

Rebecca thought that made some sense, she had never thought of that; a kind of neo-colonialism.

"I have studied many ancient accounts of pre-Christian and post-Christian philosophy and I can tell you; that although The New Testament won through. It was a close-run thing with other religious philosophies and metaphysical thought."

"You mean it's all made up?" she asked provokingly.

"No, the prophets, gurus, philosophers, great thinkers are 'legit', they must have had above average intelligence, obviously, and if they also show they have the courage to challenge 'the authorities', they of course generally attract followers, and fanatical supporters; partly because they are charismatic and partly because they show lost souls *The Way* and everyone's looking for the fucking way. I was always looking for the fucking way."

"You were playing God."

"That's ridiculous, Becky. Simon, Sotakos, The Brethren, everyone involved, wished that the main thesis of the New Testament could realise the same portent in the west as the Qur'an elicits in the east. Only a simpleton would take either tome as the *Word of God;* as your bible belt compatriots do in the US."

Rebecca could buy into that, she had met many fanatical bible bashing Americans back home who thought Darwin was the devil. And she had never considered the Roman Empire had embraced Christianity to prolong its influence. All those millions of

Roman Catholics all over the world still owing allegiance to Rome via the Vatican.

"And not even one of the dozen or so learned personages who rewrote the bible for King James were shot," Lochlan continued.

She laughed at this, melted a little, placed the gun in her lap, but held on to it, just in case she changed her mind.

"I have a question for you Lochy, which is very important to me. Do NOT give me a glib answer or I will shoot, do you copy? I want the truth that you hold so dear. The truth."

"Okay. Okay. Clearly understood. I copy."

"Dianne said, you refused to marry me." He went to say something, but she interrupted him immediately by waving the gun. "If you had gotten me pregnant, Lochy, if I had been with your child, just supposing; just supposing I was having your child. What would you have done? Would you have married me then?" He flinched, the ashen anxiety on his face returned.

"I need to know?"

"What's this all about Beck? For Christ's sake."

"Marriage is for children Lochlan, n'est ce pas? Hypothetically, just supposing, I just need to know." She raised the gun again and met his eyes.

"Okay. Okay. I would have paid for an abortion, that's the least I could do for you."

"Yes; well… well done… Sir Lochlan Majewski …you are right, that would have been the *very least* you could have done for me." Her slow, deliberation and sarcasm, was lost on him.

"Well, yes I would not have hesitated. 'Honest Indian' Becky." He pulled his 'little boy lost' expression.

"But what if I had wanted to keep *him*? Keep our baby. Marry you, live together with you as a family." He shrugged his shoulders. "I need to know Lochlan." He received the same unflinching cold stare as her uncle had when Rebecca challenged him for the absolute truth of Q. He realised, she could still shoot him.

"I would have insisted on an abortion or sued you for deception. You said you were on the pill, didn't you?" He clearly realised the irony of his statement, as he was still challenging and tried to stare defiantly back.

"I see. You never, ever, wanted children with me? Was that the problem, the reason you chose not to marry me and go for a 'barbed' substitute to gain your 30 pieces of silver?"

"Well, yes: more or less."

"What do you mean, MORE OR LESS! MORE OR LESS! What the fuck does that mean? More or less." She raised her voice again, troubling Lochlan.

"Well, Mel said you had a love thing for me and kept hinting about a '*Professor Junior*' and how you and I were the *'right age for family'* and all that; and Simon, your uncle, wanted me to marry you and keep it in the family, although I didn't realise he was related to you then. I just couldn't, not even for the Brethren's Payment. Dianne was a safe bet as I think, she's a man, almost, she's certainly not maternal, and would make no demands, or at least that's what I thought at the time. It was just an arrangement."

"Like getting a Green Card?"

"Yeah. Exactly. It wasn't my idea. I just wanted what the Brethren had promised me. You knew I wasn't sure if they would keep their word, as there was no signed contract. I just don't like children, you knew that also, Becky. They cost a small fortune, take up all of one's time and energy, and then siphon all the attention from whomsoever is your partner, towards themselves. When they finally leave the nest and it's just the two of you; then, and only then, do you get a chance to get to know each other, and fall in or out of love."

"Oh, you, poor little boy, and you want all the attention?" she said this while pouting sarcastically.

"Are you pregnant? What's this all about? Are you? You said *him*?"

"Tell you what, Mr Professor. If I *was* pregnant with your child, I would abort. You *are* a right little turd, Lochlan, you really are. I want a divorce, Lochlan Majewski. A fucking divorce."

"On what grounds?" He was goading her, for he knew, he was shit scared of taking on the responsibilities of a family and secretly admired those of his peer group, who had done so. There were even some married colleagues with several children, who had even published. Summerskill for one. *Bastards.*

"On what grounds? On what fucking grounds? On the grounds that our paper-marriage was never fucking consummated, of course."

"That's true. Although 'never fucking consummated' is tautology or something. I cannot deny it, there was no sex in our marriage. Divorce granted madam. We will just have to share out the silver then, won't we?"

At that moment the building began to vibrate as if there was a small quake. This was soon followed by a drumming throng, that developed into a roar. At first, they thought it was a helicopter landing in the private garden. Lochlan said this had happened when the PM was called away unexpectedly. Rebecca ran to the window to look towards the private garden and to her absolute delight and surprise, outside on the Terrace road was at least 30 to 40 motorbikes of the Hackney Harriers, four abreast, some static, others joining from the rear, and with their engines roaring, throbbing in unison. It was a colourful cavalcade, reminiscent of a medieval jousting event. Out in front was Shaun, in his red and black livery, astride 'Thor', his Harley Davidson, polished and gleaming. He had come to get her. They had come to get her. She was ecstatic and thrilled and buzzing with hope and everything, maybe love, yes maybe; maybe love.

"I am off Sir Lochlan, fucking, Majewski. You can stuff your pieces of silver up YOUR anus. And HERE," she said with venom as she threw the gun onto the bed, "have the gun, shoot yourself, *my dear*. I just can't be bothered."

Rebecca's dress eased up her thighs as she slid onto the pillion seat of Thor, so that she was all legs. She leant forward putting her arms around Shaun's waist, slipping her hands deep into his leather jacket pockets. The huge engine throbbed as the convoy roared off, completing a circuit of the Park Garden, whilst still four abreast, they moved off towards the Hackney High street and The Continental Café. The engine's vibrations went right through her body as she pressed down on the seat, her flesh conjoining with the pulsating leather; throbbing; pulsing; tingling; she was both relieved and excited, on a high. Oo!ere. Oo!ere. Bugger! Oh! That was nice, but very unexpected, goodness me, she thought.

Nobody, not even Dianne, who was in the same building, heard the single gunshot as the sound was muffled by the loud roar of the Harriers as they moved off. Rebecca hadn't realised that Professor Lochlan Majewski, aka, Sir Lochlan Majewski, did not suspect that the Q tablets were fake. Their most eminent Brethren, and especially Sokatos's translation (a translation that drew skilfully on the Old Testament) had convinced him of their authenticity. He could not lose face in front of Rebecca. A beautiful and intelligent woman. Who had proved to be a truly fun companion, and whom he came to love when she went missing, becoming anxious, as no one could find her and saddened, when he thought there was a possibility, he may never see Rebecca again. A love that was destroyed when he realised that she was an integral part of the scam, the woman who had set him up, and the main reason he had been so naïve. He didn't relish fame either. He just couldn't live with himself. Sir Lochlan Leonard Majewski really did believe *in the energy of the earth, the sky, nature, love, but above everything else. Truth, Honesty and Justice.*

Holding the revolver way out in front of his face, with his bandaged hand at arm's-length, holding the gun, so he could see into the barrel, Lochlan had pulled the trigger. The late Professor, Sir Lochlan Leonard Majewski had clearly understood by the precautions that he had taken when handling the gun, that Rebecca's fingerprints and DNA were all over it.

The End

CPSIA information can be obtained
at www.ICGtesting.com
Printed in the USA
BVHW040021201119
564349BV00010B/87/P